Bob Moats

I0567372

Blue Suede Murders

By Bob Moats

1

Blue Suede Murders

For information and address:
Magic 1 Productions
P.O. Box 524, Fraser MI 48026-0524
Website: http://murdernovels.com
Cover by Bob Moats

Bob Moats

Other Jim Richards series books by Bob Moats

(In Series Order)
Classmate Murders
Vegas Showgirl Murders
Dominatrix Murders
Mistress Murders
Bridezilla Murders
Magic Murders
Strip Club Murders
Made-for-TV Murders
Mystery Cruise Murders
Talk Show Murders
Sin City Murders
Black Widow Murders
Vegas Vigilante Murders
Area 51 Murders
Mortuary Murders
Hypnotic Murders
Sunshine State Murders
Blue Suede Murders
Honky Tonk Murders
Dark Carnival Murders
Lipstick Murders
Pasta Murders
Talent Show Murders
Shyster Murders
Campground Murders
Network Murders
Reunion Murders
Big Apple Murders
Kennel Murders
Trick or Treat Murders
Santa Murders
Wiseguy Murders

For a preview or to purchase a book, go to
http://murdernovels.com

What a few people are saying about Murder Novels by Bob Moats

Mr. Moats, I just got your novel "Classmate Murders" and have to let you know, I read it in one evening. That is the first book I have ever done that with. That was the most enjoyable book I have ever read. I just started reading e-books, and reading again, after getting my wife a Kindle. This book was my 12th, and the best. I just got Las Vegas Showgirls to (read) tomorrow evening. I look forward to reading many of your books in this series. I have been searching for an author and books that were fun, entertaining reads. Your books are just the ticket.

Regards, A new fan, Bill from South Carolina

****

Another very nice comment submitted through my website from Micki P.:

"I recently was given a kindle for my 60th birthday. The first book I downloaded was the Classmate Murders and have now read every one of the them. Today I started on the Fatal Rejection series. Thank you for the wonderful ride with Jim and Penny and all the rest of the troop. I have laughed and giggled thru the stories, my poor family gave me the strangest looks! Now I really want a little Yorkie!! Fatal Rejection so far is another great read! I will be looking out for more of Jim Richards and since you are my #1 Author, anything of yours I can find."

Extra special thanks to:

Thank you to all the people who purchased this book. I hope you enjoy it as much as I enjoyed writing it for my faithful readers.

The Jim Richards Family of Readers is listed in the back of the book.

Blue Suede Murders by Bob Moats

Chapter 1

Elvis hadn't left the building. Why? Because he was dead.

No, not the real Elvis, he died years ago, sitting on the toilet, or so legend or rumor has it. This Elvis wasn't the real Elvis, unless the reports of his death were greatly exaggerated. He once had been seen in Grand Rapids, Michigan working at a burger joint, but that was never proven.

This Elvis in the charred white spangled suit, was barely recognizable, he was burned severely in the pink Cadillac sitting off the Vegas strip by Sahara as the Las Vegas fire department was hosing down the flaming car while the tourists watched nearby. It was a circus for the people as they watched the car finally flame out.

When the scorched metal of the car had cooled, Vegas Metro CSI was on the scene to examine the wreck and the county medical examiner, Joesph Lang, proclaimed the body to be an impersonator. Hardly a surprise.

Lieutenant Lynn Carter, homicide detective and her partner, Sergeant Frank DeAngelo, AKA Deacon, were standing to the side waiting for the okay from the fire department to release the scorched scene. Joe

Lang said that the body was possibly doused in some type of flame accelerant and set on fire, so that's why homicide was called in.

"Hey Joe, what can you tell me?" Lynn asked Joe Lang as she was leaning over the charred remains of the classic Cadillac and looking at the body of the victim.

"Well, Elvis has left the world. He was doused in some liquid, probably kerosene from the smell or gasoline and set aflame. The fire spread to the car seats and then engulfed the whole car. The fire on the man's body probably killed him instantly, it usually does. Breathing in the flames and the lungs shut down. Poor bastard, just finished his show at Harrahs and was driving around."

"How do you know that?"

"The valet at Harrahs said he told him, just before he drove out. No one in the area saw the attack, they just saw the fire. Shame, he was so good with his impersonation."

"You know him?"

"Sure, he's the only impersonator with this model of Cadillac. Troy Berlington. Worked the impersonator show at Harrahs, I've seen him a number of times, he was good, very good. Shame he ended this way."

Deacon was listening to all this and said, "He's a hunka, hunka Burning Love now?"

Joe just gave the big man a long uncomfortable stare, shook his head and walked away. Lynn smacked his arm.

"You can be a little insensitive occasionally; didn't you see Joe had a man crush on this guy?"

"I didn't know that Joe was gay."

"Oh Deacon, he's not, he just admired the guy for his talent. Let just get through this okay?"

"Sure, I like Elvis, but I wouldn't have a crush on him."

"Shut up Deacon, let's get to work and figure out who hated Elvis enough to kill him." She went off away from the charred car and to the supervisor of the CSI.

"Paul, as soon as you get some info, let me know."

"Sure Lynn, do you have 'suspicious minds' over this killing, here 'in the ghetto'?"

"Don't you start that too, just get me the info without the song list," She huffed and walked away.

He yelled to her, "Viva Las Vegas!"

Lynn flipped him the bird and kept walking to her car followed by Deacon, trying not to laugh aloud.

~~*~~

The next morning, I rolled out of bed, nearly stepping on our toy Yorkie, Willy. He luckily shot out before my foot hit the floor and I stood. I looked around the bedroom and didn't see my lovely wife and Vegas' favorite talk show host, Penny. I listened for any sound in the house and then heard clanking from the direction of the kitchen. I was worried that Penny was making breakfast, but if it made her happy, I would force myself to eat it.

I went to my personal bathroom; it was nice we each had our own so we could get ready in the morning to go off to our respective jobs without tripping over each other. I was looking in the mirror, studying the new wrinkles showing on my face, thinking about plastic surgery.

Penny and I had just returned from a month long book tour where I signed my novels for adoring fans. Along the way, we met my book editor who was beaten and stabbed in Florida where I was meeting my readers and we ended up catching a serial killer. The best thing about the whole crime was Val, my book editor, met a nice young cop and I bought the motorhome van of my dreams.

We drove across country in the van and I now had it parked in the drive. Since it was as small as a normal van, I could drive it around and let my classic '89 Crown Vic rest in the garage. The interior of the van was as roomy as a motorhome, complete with kitchen, bathroom and bedroom. I figured that I could drive it around town and also use it as a mobile office and home away from home.

I finished up in the bathroom and headed to the kitchen ready for the worst. I turned the corner and saw Penny sitting at the snack bar watching our friend and former mob enforcer, Angelo making breakfast. I had forgotten that he was staying in our guesthouse and he loved to slip in to make us one of his famous breakfasts. I didn't object, they were very good and he enjoyed it, besides it would mean Penny wouldn't be cooking.

"Good morning everyone," I said as I came up to my wife and gave her a sloppy kiss.

"You're in a good mood this morning," she said wiping her mouth with a napkin.

I suddenly realized that she had maple syrup on her lips and I now tasted it on mine. It was good.

"I'm happy to be back home and going to my new office to set it up," I said.

Angelo came over and said, "Morning Mr. R., you sleep well?"

"I did Angelo, and thank you for watching the house while we were away."

"My pleasure, I didn't even use the pool," he said like it was an accomplishment.

"Angelo, we told you that you could use the pool if you wanted to," Penny spoke.

"I was afraid I might drown, and there'd be no one to save me."

"You could have invited someone to swim with you," I said before I realized that Angelo didn't know anyone out here. "Angelo, we have to get you some friends."

"Most the people I know are all in prison or on the run. I could join some social club but I don't think you want a bunch of wiseguys from the mob hanging around your house. We'll think of something."

I flipped on the TV to see what the forecast for weather in the Vegas valley had in store for us. There was a news reporter from Penny's station, KLAS, talking about an early morning car fire on the strip. He went on to explain that an Elvis impersonator was found in the burned out car. As the camera was scanning the scene, I caught a glimpse of Lynn and Deacon standing by the car. Penny made a little squeal of delight seeing them and laughed. Then Penny said, "Someone torched Elvis, oh that is so tragic."

I wasn't sure if she was kidding or serious.

Nearly two years ago, my beautiful wife and I flew into Vegas from Michigan to get married. We got involved in the Bridezilla murders and were almost married by an Elvis minister, much to Penny's dismay.

Blue Suede Murders

She definitely wasn't a big fan of Elvis, she never admitted it to her viewing public, she knew Elvis was revered here and didn't want hate mail. But when she found out that Elvis was to preside over our wedding she went ballistic. Luckily, Lynn had connections with a local minister from a mission in the downtown area who came in to save the ceremony. We were married on that day and were living happily ever after, so far.

Penny realized that she was supposed to be on the road to her station, so jumped up and went off to finish getting ready. I had my breakfast and thanked Angelo for it. Penny had breezed out the door saying good-bye to us and was gone. I worried that she would kill herself rushing one day.

I finished getting ready and told Angelo I was leaving. He said he had to go out and protect some recording executive today and would see us later.

I got in the van and drove out to the new building where we had moved our investigating business. It was a really nice brick and chrome building and huge. Which was good for us, now having three P.I.'s and all of Buck's one hundred and ten security guards, our last building was a bit crowded. I had only been in the building once since I got back from my tour, so I hadn't had time to set my office up. This was going to be my day to get settled in.

I drove in and parked. Going through the front door, I met with the new receptionist that Lacey hired and she remembered me from the other day when Penny and I returned to storm into the building. I walked through the second set of doors and didn't see Lacey at her desk. I walked down the hallway and into my office, I stood looking around when all of a sudden something dropped down hanging from the ceiling. It was a skeleton on a noose rope!

Lacey and Buck came into the room laughing. Buck said, "Looks like murder is following you from the old office."

*

Chapter 2

After I recovered from my minor heart attack, I managed to laugh it off. Buck got up on a chair, untied the rope holding the skeleton and handed it down to me. I was looking at the bones and saw they were plastic, but it was a full size skeleton.

"I did want an office by myself. Where did you get this thing, it looks so real?" I asked.

Lacey spoke, "I have a friend who works in the prop department at the MGM Grand theatre and they have all kinds of props for any occasion. This one was left over from Halloween. She said we could keep it, they have plenty more."

I looked over to a wall next to the door and went to find a large nail, probably left from a big picture hanging there. I pushed the end of the rope into the nail and let the skeleton hang down. I stood back and said, "It's good."

Buck plopped down on the client chair and asked, "You ready to get back to the crime grind?"

"I never got away from it. Even on my book tour, I had to contend with a serial killer. Penny is just about frazzled with all the crime going on around me. But she's holding up."

Lacey was still standing and said, "If you haven't heard about it, an Elvis impersonator was murdered early this morning after his show. Maybe something to look into."

"He had a show early this morning?"

"Well, it was last night, the show finished after midnight and then he left the casino theatre and went out for a ride. That's when he got torched," Lacey said.

"Well, Lynn and Deacon are on the case from the news report I saw this morning."

"But did you know there is going to be an Elvis convention starting this weekend?"

"No, I didn't. That's definitely not something I would put in my appointment book to see."

"If this isn't a random hit, maybe they might need investigating or protection for the other impersonators," she said with a smile.

"You are one good little P.R. person aren't you?"

"I want to see this business succeed. So I'll let you know when the Elvis people come in, I've been putting feelers out," she said, then went out of the office.

Buck laughed and said, "While you were gone Lacey was really running the office like a little dictator."

"She told me on the phone while I was away that you guys were harassing her."

"You know we love her, we only harass out of love."

"Yeah, but she doesn't take harassing well. Just don't piss her off too often. Now I have to go out to the van and get a few things I brought. By the way, where's the things from my old office, like my Penny in a bikini poster?"

"In your closet, we figured you wanted to put that stuff up yourself."

I went to the closet and opened it. I was surprised that it was almost as big inside as my last office. I picked up the box and brought it out.

Buck stood and said, "I have to go schedule next week's guard roster. I think I got myself into this too deep, too much work."

"You have to learn to delegate authority, and hire someone to do the leg work for you. You take on too much of the load by yourself."

"Yeah, I know. I'll think on it and maybe find someone to do it." He went out and I was finally alone. Well, I had the skeleton to keep me company.

About an hour later, I had the poster up along with all my wall decorations and pictures. I put up the plaques of the bullets that were removed from my body from past cases and hung on the wall as souvenirs, to remind me of how dangerous this job could be. I was happy that I had no bullets from Penny to hang up, and I wasn't going to let anyone start to provide me with them.

I went to my big walnut desk and sat admiring the thing. The lawyers had left most of the furniture when they cleared out. They weren't a happy bunch from what I understood. I was leaning back in my chair when I saw up in the corner of the room, by the ceiling, a camera. I stood and went around the desk and got up on a chair to get a closer look. It definitely was a camera.

I was out in the hallway trying to figure where the cable from the camera led to. Earl came out of his office and saw me.

"Hey Jim, what's up?"

"Do you know there is camera in my office?"

"Sure, they're in all the offices. You have a lot to learn about this place. Come on, I'll show you the security room." He led me to the back of the building and into a small room that had monitors and recording boxes on one wall.

16

"We can monitor any room as long as the person in that room doesn't shut off the camera with a button under the desks. Nice security feature."

"I feel so violated." I laughed. "Does Trapper know about this?"

"Sure, he's been playing with it since we found it. He spies on Lacey and the new girl up front, just for fun."

"Well, tell Lacey about it, I don't want her to freak out knowing we've been watching her."

"Spoil sport," Earl laughed.

"Now, any other surprises I should know about?"

"Nope that's all the subversive things they had in here."

I was looking at the monitor and saw Buck laying back in his chair sleeping. I laughed and said, "I wish I could say something to him from here."

"You can, oh that's right I forgot, there are public address speakers in each office." He pointed to a microphone and said, "Press the button and I'll open the speaker in Buck's office."

"Does Buck know about this?"

"He knows about the cameras but not the speakers. I just discovered them two days ago, before I went home. Go ahead, say something."

Blue Suede Murders

I grinned, pressed the microphone button and said in a deep booming voice, "BUCK! This is God, you do not sleep while working, it is forbidden!"

We both roared when Buck shot up from his chair and was looking around the room. He came around the desk and we could see him looking up and down, then under his desk.

I boomed again, "BUCK CARSON! Do not tempt the fates, you are going to work and like it! I have a mission for you!"

We saw him go out of the office. I told Earl to cut the feed and we went out of the room. We met him in the hall and he was looking a shade of white.

He saw Earl and I trying to keep from laughing.

"Okay, what the hell is going on?" he roared.

"Why Buck, whatever do you mean?" I asked.

Then Earl and I lost it, we both roared with laughter. Buck just looked frustrated and went back to his office, but before he went in, he turned and said, "Just stop it, not funny!" He went in and slammed the door.

I looked down the hallway to the front lobby through the glass doors and saw something I wasn't prepared for, three Elvises standing at the counter talking to Lacey.

"Oh crap, they're invading now." I said and Earl turned to see what I was talking about.

"Well you can take care of them, I'm not an Elvis fan," he said then went back to his office. I heard a voice over the P.A. calling for me. Great, Lacey has a microphone too. I was heading up to the lobby when Buck popped back out of his office.

"Are you guys still playing with that thing?"

"No, it's Lacey now. I guess she has a microphone up at her desk also." Buck saw the Trio of Elvises and followed me out.

I went around the back of the counter, looked under the counter top to the desk and saw she had monitors also. "You knew about the cameras?" I asked.

"Sure, Earl told me about them just after we moved in. I"ve been spying on Trapper spying on me," she laughed.

"I'll have to have a talk with Earl. Now what can I do for you gentlemen?" I asked of the lead Elvis.

"We need protection and someone to investigate the death of one of our brothers," the young, leather jacketed Elvis said.

"I can see the protection, but aren't the police investigating the death that happened this morning."

Blue Suede Murders

"Yes, but we don't feel the police will give this a priority." The later in life, fat Elvis said. His white jumpsuit and the spangles glittered in the light coming in from the skylights. "And we have a convention to contend with, four days of activities."

I was trying not to laugh at these men dressed up like various years of the icon of rock and roll. They reminded me of the flying Elvis' from the movie, jumping out of a plane with parasails over Las Vegas.

"I happen to know the Detectives who are handling the case and they are very dedicated officers. I'm sure they will take care of the murder for you. Did you know the deceased?"

"Everyone knew him, he was a great performer, he had all of Elvis' moves down to perfection. We are worried now because there have been rumors that this is not going to be the first death in our group. Some of our brothers have been threatened and we are not happy Elvises."

"We can provide you with protection," I said and looked to Buck, he nodded, "We have numerous bodyguards that we can put at your disposal. Why don't you follow my associate to his office and you can discuss the needs of your people."

Before they could go, the front lobby door opened and in came Lynn and Deacon. Lynn saw the Elvis' and just said, "Damn."

*

Chapter 3

I took Lynn and Deacon into my new office, they just stood and looked around, then Lynn screamed when she saw the skeleton.

"Damn woman, I thought you were a tough Vegas cop?" I said.

"I hate skeletons, I've always hated skeletons ever since I was a child and my father sent me into a haunted house by myself. I'll never forgive him for that. They had all these skeletons dancing around, it was debilitating."

"So skeletons and spiders, anything else we need to know about?" I asked.

"Thanks for bringing up spiders again." She glanced at the skeleton again and shivered.

Deacon was already seated and trying not to laugh. Lynn whacked him on the head and sat. I went to my chair behind my desk and sat down. "So what brings you here?"

"I need to have someone check all these Elvises for me. I don't have the people to do it or the time. I figured you can snoop around and the city would pay you as a civilian advisor. Want to make some money or do you have a lot of customers beside the Elvises?"

Blue Suede Murders

I sat looking to the skeleton thinking he needed an identity, then said, "I can investigate the imposters, what do you have so far on the murder?"

"I'll give you the murder book we have started to look over, he was an employee of Harrahs entertainment division, but we believe that a rival impersonator is behind this, there's just too damn many of them in Vegas to investigate all of them. Especially with the convention, so you're hired."

"You expect me to talk to hundreds of Elvises?"

"Gee, you catch on fast, do you want the job?"

I thought about the men in Buck's office. I could take their case to find the killer, taking the same case as the civilian advisor job from the police and double the income. I smiled and said, "Deal."

"I'm not trusting you for some reason?" Lynn said.

"What? You came here to ask me to take the case. What's the problem?"

"I don't know, but I'll find out. I'll send over Warren with the info you will need. Just keep me filled in; Captain Weber is expecting results. He is a big fan of Elvis, so you are expected to get results fast."

I cringed thinking that Weber was a fan of Elvis. "Okay, I'll be on it."

Lynn stood followed by Deacon. He was such a puppy when it came to Lynn, I thought of her being the husband and Deacon being the wife if they got married. That was not a good image of Deacon in a bride's wedding gown. I shook my mind to get it out.

"Okay, I'll watch for the info and get on this ASAP," I said.

"I'll be watching you, so get me some results," she paused, then said, "Please."

"I'll do my amazing best, you can count on me."

They went out and I walked down the hall to Buck's office. I entered and went to the lead Elvis.

"Do you still want us to find the killer?" I asked.

"Sure we do, this is not good for our people if we are being killed off. When can you start?"

"I just did, now tell me everything about your convention."

We spent about an hour talking about the activities of the convention and I was taking notes. Buck was on his phone calling in six of his biggest guards to handle the protection of the Elvises who were threatened. I finished with the info and told them we would be out in the morning to start our protection and investigation. The young leather jacketed Elvis said his name was Morgan and I gave him my card to call if he needed us before tomorrow.

Blue Suede Murders

The men all thanked us and left. I sat with Buck and thought about how we could take on this account.

"Do your men have any training in protection?" I asked.

"While you were gone I had Angelo do a few training classes in handling the enemy, namely the criminals. Angelo is really good at the leg breaking and getting to know the enemy. I have six good men who I think would be great at the body guarding."

"Okay, we have that covered. Now I need to do some talking to all the Elvises to see where they stand on the murder. This is going to be complicated." I stood and started to go out.

"What are you going to do now?" Buck asked.

"I need to go give a friend an identity." I went out leaving Buck wondering.

An hour later, Buck came into my office to tell me that he had his men ready to go to work. I smiled and was looking behind him. He turned to see the skeleton now sitting on a chair, with a cigar in it's jaws, glasses and a base ball cap on sideways.

Buck roared and asked where I got the props.

"There was a box of lost and found that Lacey told me about. I got the items out of there. He is now to be respected and called, well... I don't have a name for him yet, but I'll work on it. For now he is to be referred to as Mr. Bones."

"I like," Buck said and finished telling me about his men.

"I'm putting them in the purple blazers I bought and they will be standing tall for inspection at zero-six-hundred hours tomorrow morning. I called Angelo to come in to give a pep talk to them."

"Works for me. I'm not looking forward to interviewing hundreds of Elvises, but it has to be done. Who is Angelo guarding now?"

"He's going to be watching some computer whiz kid at a geek convention and protecting his million dollar ass from competitors."

"Ah, the matrix game plot. Is Angelo prepared for the computer world of gaming?" I said knowing that there was a big convention of computer game manufacturers in town.

"He said he is, but I don't know how well he will handle a fifteen year old kid. I hope he doesn't kill the kid or go brain dead. Angelo is good but he's not the brightest bulb in the marquee."

"Just keep an eye on him and help him. He'll learn quickly."

Lacey knocked on my door and I said to come in. She said there was a woman in the lobby needing help. I said I'd be out in a minute. Buck stood and said he was going back to work and left. I got up and went to the lobby and found a woman, rather plain but attractive in a plain way, standing at the counter.

Blue Suede Murders

"May I help you? I'm Jim Richards."

"Yes, I need help to find a husband."

I was married so I felt safe, "What do you mean, Miss..."

"I'm Rebecca Walker, and I have a fiancé who disappeared yesterday. We were going to be married in two days but he's vanished. It's not like him, so I figured he's in trouble. The police won't help until he's been gone for forty-eight hours, but we are scheduled to be married by then. So you can see my quandary."

"Yes, I see. Can you wait for a minute?"

She said she would and I went back to Earl's office. He was sitting back relaxing as I went to his desk and said, "I have a woman who is looking for a lost fiancé. He probably is out sobering up or having a case of cold feet, but can you take it, I'm going to be questioning Elvises tomorrow. Or you could take the Elvis questioning."

"Oh no, I don't get along with Elvises, they scare me."

"Mr. big black ops guy afraid of Elvises? Now I'm worried."

"Well don't be. I had a run in with a team of foreign enemy agents all disguised as Elvises back when I was with the CIA and they tortured me in unspeakable ways. So I don't play well with them."

I stood for a minute then said, "You're making that up. You know I have to talk to a hundred or so Elvises and you don't want to be involved."

"No, really I was tortured by them. I hated every minute of it. Really."

"Okay you have the missing groom, go talk to her." I turned and went out. Earl came down the hallway and out to the lobby where he met the woman and took her back to his office.

I was back at my desk laughing at Earl's lame attempt to avoid having to do a lot of grunt work. I'd have to remember the story he made up. Lacey went by my office and I called to her. She came back.

"Where's Trapper off to?" I asked.

"Didn't I tell you, he's taking a week off to go somewhere with his lady friend Sam. He said he'd be back soon."

"Thanks," I said and she went off. Now I felt alone in this Elvis case. I had hoped to pawn off some of the work to Trapper, but it looks like I'm on my own.

I looked up to the camera in the corner of the room and noticed the little red light was on. I started to feel under my desk for this button Earl told me about. I got out of my chair and looked around for it, but couldn't find it. I was just about ready to call Lacey when a voice boomed out, "Richards! God orders you to get busy!"

The voice sounded strangely like Buck.

*

Chapter 4

Earl walked into my office as I was on the ground looking under my desk. He stopped at the middle of the room and watched me. I suddenly saw him standing there and came up too fast, hitting my head on the edge of the desk.

"Ouch, you okay?" Earl asked.

"I'd be better if I could find that lousy button for the camera you told me about," I said rubbing my head.

He came around the back of the desk, opened the side drawer and pointed to a button on the inside of the drawer.

"Well, you didn't say it was in the drawer, you just said under it," I said as I walked around him to look, then pushing the button and saw that the little red light was out on the camera.

"I also didn't tell you that Lacey can monitor the building and make calls over the P.A., I like having fun with you."

"Well, stop it. I have enough problems without you compounding them. Now are you going to help the dismayed bride?"

"You know I had that case of the missing bridesmaid just before you went on your book tour. Why am I getting all these nuptial cases?"

"What is Las Vegas well known for? Gambling, big stage shows and getting married. There are a good number of men, and women who get cold feet and decide to hide rather than tell their fiancé that they don't want to get married. I'll bet if you check the airport, you'll find this woman's fiancé has flown the coop."

"The last woman I tracked down wasn't fleeing from a wedding, she was kidnapped."

"I know, I was starting to write a book about it."

Earl looked to me and paused, "You actually were going to write about my exploits. I'll have to kill you if you give away my secret past."

"What, that you are a top secret black ops CIA spook and you have overthrown countries and dictators?"

"Right, so be careful what you say."

"Go do some investigating and let me get to work on my Elvis case. Or do you want to help?"

"No, I have chills just thinking about Elvis. Waterboarding wasn't a fun experience."

Blue Suede Murders

"The evil Elvises waterboarded you?"

"Well they weren't baptizing me," he said with a laugh and went out of the room.

"I'm surrounded by crazies," I mumbled to myself.

"Richards!! Get to work!!" Buck's barely disguised voice boomed again over the speakers. I went out and down to the security room, finding Buck sitting at the monitor desk. I came up and grabbed the microphone, unplugging it and took it with me out of the room. Buck just laughed aloud.

I was coming back down the hallway when I saw the new girl, Tracey, coming towards me. Tracey and Lacey, now that was odd.

"Mr. Richards, there are two people in the front lobby who want to see you," she said.

"Why didn't you just page me?"

"Lacey took my microphone away, she said I was annoying her with it. I was just using it to say there were people in the front who wanted to see our detectives. But she said I didn't have the voice for it."

I could understand that, Tracey had a droning voice, bland and monotonous. "Well thank you for telling me. I'll be up in a minute. Oh, and next time you can use the phone to call Lacey and she can chase me down."

She thanked me and went back out to her desk as I put the microphone that I took from Buck in my office. Now we had taken two microphones away from people who shouldn't have access to them. I went out and to the main lobby where I found a big surprise.

"Val, Blake what are you two doing here?" I said to my book editor and her boy toy cop who Penny and I met out in Florida in the last month. They were part of our having to take down a serial killer and Val had been kidnapped by him. Blake was a cop in that town who Val took a shine to and he helped to rescue her.

"Jim, good to see you again," Val said as she gave me a big hug. I shook Blake's hand and then asked them to come into my office. We went through the doors to the inner lobby and I stopped to introduce them to Lacey.

We went to my office and I had them sit. "Now why are you out here in Vegas?"

"Blake and I have never been here and we wanted to see it along with you and Penny. Also we decided to get married here," she said with a big smile on her face, I was a bit shocked.

"Wow, that was quick, you two just met less than a month ago."

"Well, you know how you always said in your books that I edited, you knew when you met Penny that it was the right thing. We feel the same way." I looked to Blake and he was grinning like a kid on Christmas day.

Blue Suede Murders

"Yes, but I knew Penny from high school many years ago, so I sort of knew about her after all these years. But I'm not one to judge, I hope you guys are happy. Have you made any plans yet, for the wedding I mean?"

"Nope, we jest decided ta come out and git married. Ah am delighted to be here with ma future wife." Blake spoke finally in that southern accent that annoyed the hell out of me while we out there. I had hoped I never heard it again.

"Okay, I'm sure Penny will be delighted also. I'll call her after she is finished with her TV show and let her know you are here. Do you have a place to stay?"

"We're in a motel just outside of the city. It's cheap and near enough to get into town."

"How did you come out, plane or drive?"

"We flew, then caught a cab at the airport to take us to a cheap motel. I had a good deal of money stashed away and Blake had a lot of bonds that he cashed so we could come out. We got a cab from the motel to here."

"I'd offer you our guesthouse but it's being used at the moment," I said then paused, "Listen, once the dust settles, I'm putting you two up in the MGM Grand, the honeymoon suite. No arguments, just take it as a wedding gift from Penny and I."

"Oh we won't argue, that's mighty nice of y'all," Blake said with his baby-faced grin.

"Okay, now have you eaten?"

"No and we are starved, the plane only had crackers. Such a shame for the price one pays to fly," Val laughed. "We went straight to the motel then back here, so we haven't eaten yet."

"Good, hold on a minute." I pulled out my cell phone and dialed Penny's cell. I checked with the clock and she should have been done at her studio. I didn't know where she was but knew she'd answer when she saw it was me. I could hear the phone ring a few times through my cellphone, then I heard a ringing from the hallway and Penny walked into my office. She didn't see our guests because they had their backs to the door.

She smiled and said, "I saw it was you, so I didn't answer." Val turned to her and Penny stopped with her mouth open. "Val what are you doing here? And Blake, good to see you again."

I stood and said, "We'll explain it to you over lunch, my treat, shall we go?"

We all went out to the van and piled in. Val said, "I see you still have this thing."

"Yes, it's my baby now."

Penny said, "I thought I was your baby?"

"You know what I mean. You're my babe, this is my baby."

Blue Suede Murders

We drove over to Bistros Restaurant and went in to be seated. Val explained to Penny the reason they were in town and Penny was bouncing over it all.

"Wow, how are you planning on the ceremony?"

"We just figured that we'd go to one of those wedding chapels on the main road and get married."

"Oh no you're not, I'm going to call my wedding planner Shelby Francis and have her set it up for you. My treat."

Val was looking a bit teary eyed and I said, "Blake, how much time off from the police do you have?"

"Ah took a leave of absence, so there's no time limit, jest back to work when we return."

"Good because Penny will make this a long event."

She gave me a whack to my arm and said to behave.

"I have an important case now, so Penny may have to entertain you for a few days, but I'll be around. Blake would you like to tail me and help me track down a killer again?"

His eyes went big and said, "Ah shore would like that. Much obliged."

"Penny and Val can go visit Shelby and get the wedding plans started. I'll have to throw you a bachelor party, Vegas style."

Val spoke, "Just don't get him involved with any Vegas strippers, he's too innocent."

I laughed and said, "We can party without corrupting him, just you worry about the wedding ceremony and I'll get him safely back to you in one piece."

We finished our meal and went out to the van. Blake asked, "What is this case y'all got?"

I said, "We are going to catch the killer of Elvis."

He stopped and just dropped his mouth and stared at me.

*

Chapter 5

"You mean... but I thought he died from drugs!!?? He was murdered?? And you have a lead??" Blake was breathless.

"Take a breath Blake and quiet down, not the real Elvis, just an impersonator who was murdered last night. Just don't say anything yet, especially to Penny, she hates Elvis."

"I won't say anything, wow, Elvis is dead," he said and got into the van behind the women. I just shook my head.

35

Blue Suede Murders

I dropped the women off at the office by Penny's car. She was going to take Val to see Shelby Francis and get the wedding plans made. I told Blake to stay with me.

"The last time Penny was in Shelby's bridal salon, there were murders. So I think we'll just stay away."

"Val isn't in danger is she?" Blake said sounding worried.

"No, relax, she's safe, but then again, Penny planning a wedding can be scary. Now we have to go find out who killed Elvis."

"Y'all said that, what Elvis are ya referring to?"

"It's an impersonator, they have tons of them out here and one got cooked in his car the other night. I was asked to help the police by talking to as many Elvis impersonators as I can stomach. Plus, there's a convention of Elvis impersonators in town, so this place will have them coming out the ass."

Blake laughed and said, "Ah've only seen an Elvis impersonator once, he was okay. Didn't have the moves though."

"Well, we will be up to our noses in them, so you will be able to see a good number. Probably even see a few performing."

I drove over to the MGM Grand where the convention was being held and parked. The van slipped nicely into the space in the parking structure.

I stayed in the van, pulled my cell phone out and dialed the young leather jacketed Elvis, real name Morgan, and he answered.

"Morgan, Jim Richards here, we are in the building, no pun intended, and need to see you."

"Mr. Richards you're early, I thought you said in the morning."

"I had some time to use and decided it would be better used here. Where are you?"

"I'm in the concert hall setting up for the competition; just ask any employee where the hall is for the Elvis performances."

"See you shortly then," I said and hung up. I looked to Blake and said, "Thank ya, thank ya verry much," in my worst impersonation of Elvis.

Blake laughed and we left the van. We took the walkways down to the main floor and into the building. I found a security guard and asked where the Elvis hall was. He grinned and said to follow the flow of sparkly suits, pointing down an offshoot of the lobby. I saw what he meant. There were a couple dozen Elvises all decked out in vintage costumes from Elvis' early leather days with tight jeans and white sox to the more modern Elvis in the spangled jumpsuits. They were everywhere.

Blake was walking with his mouth opened. "Blake close your mouth, you look like a star struck kid. If you are going to investigate with me you have to turn on your cop instinct and act like a detective."

"Yas sir, Mr. Richards. Ah'll conduct myself in a professional manner."

"And stop calling me Mr. Richards, we've been through chasing down a serial killer together, you can call me Jim."

"Thank ya, Jim."

I really need to get this boy to grow up. I hope Val will help with that. My cell phone rang just outside the entrance to the hall; I saw it was Penny.

"Hey babe, what's up? No murders at Shelby's I hope."

"No, just checking to see if you two aren't getting into trouble."

"Nope, just going in to see your favorite performer, Elvis. And there are about a couple hundred of them walking around here, it's spooky."

"Well, you can keep them. I didn't know that you were investigating the murder, you kept awful mum about it."

"I would have told you, but I didn't have the time. Lynn asked me to help a short time before Val and Blake showed up. I didn't think our lunch was the appropriate place to discuss murder, and I know you don't care for Elvis, so I just kept it to myself."

"Thank you for that, please don't bring any Elvises home with you. If you do, you'll be sleeping outside."

"Last thing on my mind. How's everything with Shelby?"

"All's well, Val is trying on gowns now."

"Are you personally paying for the entire wedding?"

"We can split it. Between the two of us we could buy the chapel and marry people. Now there's a new business for you."

"I may be an ordained minister of the Universal Life Faith Church, credentials purchased online, but I have no intentions of marrying people. Not my thing. So have fun, I have to go question a few hundred Elvi, plural. That sounds like a disease."

"It is Sweetie, it is." She hung up and I put my phone away. I looked at Blake and thought we would need to get him a tuxedo. I wondered if he ever wore one before and asked.

"Oh sure, ah wore a tux when ma cousin got married and he asked me to stand fer him."

I wondered if his cousin was marrying another cousin, I didn't ask.

"Good, we need to go get you one for your wedding." I turned and went to the hall entrance; we were stopped by the men taking tickets.

"I'm here at the request of Morgan Taylor, head Elvis I guess. I'm investigating the death of Troy Berlington," I said as showed him my ID. He smiled and said to go to the left and Morgan was there by the judges table.

I led Blake down the long aisle to the front where I could see a table set up for five persons, all now seated. I recognized a couple as local celebrities from the TV and newspapers. I came up to the table and one man I knew, Nolan Clark, from the Review-Journal newspaper saw me. He yelled to me, "Jimmy are you entering the competition?"

"Oh hell no, Penny would kill me. Good to see they roped you into judging." I saw Morgan and he saw me, and then came over.

I shook his hand as he said, "Good of you to come. Why don't you relax a bit and watch the first round of entrants to get a feel for what we do here."

"Sure, just one question, was Troy Berlington supposed to be in this competition?"

"Yes he was, as a matter of fact. In the later years Elvis segment, which is later tomorrow."

"Is there a prize for this?"

"Well, there's a contract to perform at the Tropicana and a grand prize of $10,000 dollars. Excuse me, I have to get everyone ready."

"Sure we'll talk later," I said and led Blake to seats

behind the judges. We sat and then the lights in the room went dark.

We endured an hour of the jail house rock Elvises, and the men went through all the gyrations and pelvic thrusts. Blake was entranced by it all, I was barely holding on.

After the judges gave up their decision as to the best one on stage, the audience was applauding and standing for the winner. As much as I wasn't a fan of Elvis, I had to admit they were good. All but one, some overweight guy who couldn't sing a note if his life depended on it. I was amazed he even thought he was good.

I looked over to Blake who was taking in all the bright lights and glamour of it all. Poor man, he lived in the backwoods of Florida and never experienced the bright lights of the big city, especially Las Vegas. Where everything was big.

We watched the contestants standing on stage accepting their awards, it was nice that they gave everyone a trophy, smaller than the big winner, but never the less a trophy. I had participated in a number of talent contests doing my comedy magic act, and never came away with a trophy, much less a certificate.

The show ended and I went to Morgan standing off the side as he was talking to some person who was a judge. I waited and then heard them argue about something and the man stomped off. Morgan turned and saw me; he came over.

"Mr. Richards, how do you want to start this?" he asked.

"Well, first, who do you think had the most to lose if Troy participated in the competition?"

He paused and gave it a bit of thought, then he said, "I would say Charles Lawton. He does jumpsuit Elvis also and he was the second favorite after Troy. You don't think he could have done it?"

"I don't have any idea until I talk to people. So can you point out this Lawton to me?"

Morgan stood looking around the floor of the theatre and then said, "Yes, I see him." He pointed to a man in an outlandish white and silver jumpsuit with a collar that nearly covered his head from the sides. He had on sunglasses that were oversized, he looked like a caricature more than a tribute to Elvis. I thanked Morgan and went to Lawton, coming up behind him followed by Blake.

He was talking to some man in a suit and then they finished. The suited man walked off leaving Lawton alone. I tapped him on his shoulder and he jumped just about out of his jumpsuit.

I said, "Sorry, I didn't mean to scare you."

"It's all right, I'm just a bit jumpy because I was threatened with death."

*

Chapter 6

I was watching the man walk away, "Who's the suit?" I asked.

Lawton looked back and then said, "He's my manager. He's not happy with the way things are going on here. And you are?"

"I'm sorry, my name is Jim Richards, I own Richards Investigations and Security. You will be getting a bodyguard if you feel threatened. I'm also investigating the death of Troy Berlington. Do you know the man?"

"Of course, we all knew each other; he is a brother in our cause, to keep the legend of Elvis alive. I was shocked to learn he was killed."

"Are you from Vegas?"

"No, I live in LA, and come out here occasionally to perform. That's how I knew Troy."

"You said you were threatened, how did you receive the threat?" I asked.

"My wife answered the phone yesterday and she said a voice warned me that I was going to die if I didn't pull out of the competition. The caller hung up and that was all. Frightened the hell out of my wife, because she knows I would never pull out. I just need to be extra cautious now."

"As I said my firm has been hired to protect the performers who felt threatened, I'll assign a man to be your bodyguard."

"I don't think that will be necessary Mr. Richards, I don't take threats lightly. Like Elvis, I carry guns."

"Yes, but Elvis also had bodyguards, his posse."

"True, it may be nice to have a posse of my own, wouldn't it?"

"Makes you look good, like you need protection from the adoring fans."

He thought a moment, "Okay, put one of your men on me, I'll go with it for now. Maybe keep my wife happy with someone watching my back."

"I'll have one of our biggest men on you shortly, to make you look good."

"Thank you Mr. Richards, good to know you are on the scene. I'll spread the word to see if anyone else has been threatened."

I handed him my card and said, "If you need anything, here's my number."

He thanked me again and said he had some errands to do and walked away. I turned to Blake standing behind me taking it all in.

"Well Blake, what do you think?"

"Ah am amazed, they all look so good in their outfits."

"Not that, did you hear what he said?"

"Shore did, his wife took the threat. He hasn't been informed personally."

"Right, would you take that as something to worry about."

"Ah would never think to question Val if'n she said I was threatened."

"Of course, Val would crush you if you did. But I'm the kind of person who would want to hear it myself. I think Lawton is the same. That's why he's not taking it seriously."

I pulled my cell phone and called Buck. He came on and I said, "Hey, I'm at the Elvis convention, can you send a couple of the men over, I have at least one Elvis who was threatened."

"I can do that. Three of the men are still here, I'll send them and have them call you when they get there."

"Great, I'll be questioning people till then." We finished and disconnected.

"Blake, shall we go talk to a few more Elvises?"

Blue Suede Murders

We went back to Morgan as he was talking to a spangled Elvis. He turned his head to see me and finished his talk, coming to Blake and me.

"I'm getting a few more Elvises who say they were threatened. What the hell is going on? Who would want to murder Elvis?"

I thought of saying my wife but held my tongue. "That's what I intend to find out. Is there a room that these men could gather so I can dig some more? Also, to set up protection."

"I'll arrange it and call you. Now I have to go get the festivities running for the sales booths. Elvis is a big seller and the Elvis estate is getting rich." He smiled and went off.

I took Blake up to the reception hall where they had all the booths set up. I thought about buying Penny an Elvis t-shirt but I didn't want to incur her wrath. Oh hell, I bought one anyway, just to get her blood pressure up. This one had an early Elvis shaking it and the text said, "I'm a Hunka-Hunka Burning Love for You". I knew that would get her.

Blake said, "Val is a big fan of Elvis, she even wants ta git married by him."

I stopped in my tracks and looked to him, "Is she serious?"

"She shore is, ah don't care if'n it makes her happy, and it's all legal. Kin Elvis marry people?"

"Oh yes he can, and I'm wondering how Penny is going to take knowing that." I thought about when Shelby arranged our marriage ceremony and she had an Elvis to preside, Penny went crazy and luckily we found another minister through Lynn. I'd probably hear about it when I got home.

"Okay Blake, good luck to you. Hey, who's your best man going to be?"

"Well, I was goin' ta ask y'all but Val said she wanted you to walk her down the aisle. So ah don't have anyone yet. Don't tell Val I tole y'all about the walking thing."

"I won't, I'll wait till she asks, but we need to get you a best man. I'll think on it." My cell phone buzzed and I saw it was unknown, I answered. "Hello?"

"Jim, it's Morgan and I got most of the Elvises who were threatened in a conference room called OZ. Ask any of the hotel people where it is. I think the name is from the Wizard of Oz, the MGM movie since we are in the MGM Grand."

"Got ya, I'll find it." We hung up and I took Blake to the hallway and asked a porter the directions. He took us there and we went in to find a room containing about ten Elvises of different generations. Some were good looking, some were ridiculous looking and there was one Elvis in a white jumpsuit, I swear, had to be twelve years old. I went to him.

"Aren't you a little young to be Elvis." The kid stood and swiveled his hips, struck a pose, arm and fingers extended and said, "Thank ya, thank ya very much, I am young but I am good at this."

I was seriously trying not to laugh, I was about to bust a gut when Morgan came up.

"Jim, this is Danny Boorton, he's well known in our ranks as a rising star. His mother told me that she got a threat too, so I included him."

"I see, thanks, I have bodyguards coming in, but I think I may need to have more come. Excuse me," I said and went to the side of the room and called Buck again.

He came on, "This is getting serious, I need reinforcements, about ten guards or more if you have them."

"I'll call up the Marines and send them in," he said and hung up.

I turned to Blake and said, "What the hell, why is this getting so crazy? All these people being threatened just because they impersonate Elvis. I really need to dig."

I went to the front of the room where there was a podium and found a microphone, it was live, so I called everyone's attention.

"Good afternoon, I'm Jim Richards of Richards Investigations and Security, and I was hired to try and protect all of you. I have men coming in to act as bodyguards for those who feel unsafe. I was also asked by the Las Vegas Metro Police homicide to help track down the killer of Troy Berlington and I need to talk to each of you to see if there's a connection. I hope you all will cooperate and make this swift and get you back to your convention. Now just sit and be patient and things will run smoothly."

A half hour later Buck's guards had shown up and I was assigning them to various Elvises who asked for protection. I set up a table to question everyone. I called over the closest Elvis and he sat.

He looked a bit ridiculous in his fake pompadour hair, sunglasses and the overdone jumpsuit. I was waiting for it to light up and aid planes in landing.

"Your name please?" I asked cautiously.

"Don't you have to read me my rights?" he asked.

"No, I'm not the police and you are not under arrest or a suspect, I just need you to answer a few questions for me. Is that all right with you?"

"I'd like to be given my rights."

I sat staring at this man and wondering what his major malfunction was. "Okay, you have the right to be quiet, you don't have to incriminate yourself and you can have a lawyer, but if you do, you will look guilty, so do you agree to talk now?"

He grinned and said, "Okay."

"Now you say you were threatened, how did you receive the threat?"

"I heard it from the voices in my head. I have psychic powers you know. I can talk to Elvis, the King, also. He comes to me late at night and we talk. I heard the voice say I was going to die."

I was about to smack him, but held on. "Okay when did you hear this voice telling you that you would die?"

"Yesterday just after I heard about Troy's death in the fire. The voice said to me, Merle, that's my name, you are going to die too."

"Well, thank you for that. I'll need to investigate that later, but you can go for now, thanks."

He stood and shook my hand. I saw Buck come in and called to him. "Jimmy, how's it going?"

I shook my head and said, "This is going to be crazier than I thought."

*

Chapter 7

Buck pulled up a chair next to me and stretched out. I filled him in on what transpired while I was there. He got a kick out of the Elvis wanting his rights read and hearing voices.

"Sounds like the boy has a few bats nesting around that high hair of his," Buck said with a grin.

"Yep, want to listen in on a few more interviews?"

"Line them up, I think I'll enjoy this."

I called over the next Elvis, this one had a Foo Manchu type mustache and was wearing a side shooter, looked like a Colt Revolver. He sat and gave us a stern glare. Okay nut job number two.

"Hi, what's your name?"

"Jimmy Bob Maxwell, ah be from Texas, son."

Great another southerner mangling the language. "Okay and you say you were threatened, how?"

"Ah got a phone call, the hombre says ah'll go down if'n I git in the contest. I think not."

"Why's that?"

"Cause ah got ma faithful six shooter." He pulled the gun from its holster and spun it on his finger. The gun went off busting out a window on a door and everyone screamed and dove for the floor.

Two of Buck's guards were standing behind the man talking when the gun went off and they both dove for the man grabbing the gun and the man's family jewels. He howled and let the gun go. They brought him up as I yelled that it was all right to the people in the room. Buck took the gun and said he'd hold onto it, then removed the bullets.

"Ah'm mighty sorry about that, son. Got stuck on ma finger."

Two very big, armed security guards from the hotel came rushing in, we explained the situation and they took the flustered Elvis out to be questioned as to why he had a loaded gun in the center.

I sat back down and wanted to put my head on the table and weep. This was not going well. Buck was chuckling to himself and Blake said that it was interesting. I looked to him and said, "How interesting would it have been if he shot you instead of the window?"

"Not a good thing ah guess."

"Right," I said and wondered if the next loony was worth the effort. I'd recommend to Lynn to lock up the whole bunch of them. I called the next one, a young good-looking Elvis in leather and jeans. He had real hair piled up like Elvis and had a sneer like the king.

"Interesting day so far wouldn't you say?" I asked him.

"Naw, I've seen worse. Get all these posers in one place and the pandemonium just starts. I'm a serious tribute artist of the King, I don't take just it to heart, I live it."

I studied him for a second than realized he was the

performer who won the morning competition, Kent Downing.

"Congratulations Kent on winning the show this morning."

"Thank ya," he said cooly.

"Now, you were threatened like these others, how did you find out?"

"I got a phone call this morning warning me I better stay away or else."

"Or else what?"

"He didn't say, just hung up. I wasn't impressed or frightened so I'm here."

"You refused a bodyguard, don't you think that is a little dangerous in light of the threat?"

"Naw, I'm alright. I've had training in martial arts, just like Elvis. I'm a Ninth Dan Red Belt. I fear no man, or woman, they can be just as dangerous."

"Yes, you haven't met my wife," I said then asked, "Why would you think someone would threaten so many performers?"

"Jealousy, hate, revenge, trying to get ahead of others by eliminating the competition. So many things."

"Very good, you aren't by chance a detective are you?"

"No, I'm a criminal lawyer, from New York."

"Ah, you probably need the martial arts then."

"It helps. I have no idea why the threats, but this is not over."

"Why?"

"Someone is trying to make a point and so far no one is taking Berlington's death seriously. There will be another death."

His statement gave me a slight chill, like he knew something he wasn't telling. I'd have to put a big star next to his name.

"Well thank you for your input, Kent, if you hear anything more let me know," I said as I handed him my card. I didn't like lawyers but it was a good idea to keep them on your side.

He stood and nodded, then went off. I looked to Buck, "Think he may be right about another killing?"

"It would make sense, depending on the killer's goal in this."

"Yep, I'm hoping he fulfilled his goal with Berlington, but I don't think he's done either."

~~*~~

"You want who to perform your wedding?" Penny howled when Val revealed her decision to have Elvis preside over the wedding.

"Elvis, I always loved it on TV when the ceremony is done with Elvis in Vegas. It's so Vegas wedding. I want the whole burning love theme, with the vows of never going to the heartbreak hotel again.

"You're not serious," Penny grumbled.

"Sure, that's what I want. Shelby can you arrange it?"

Shelby stood not knowing what to say, she had arranged for Penny's wedding to have Elvis and that came out bad. Penny just waited for Shelby to speak.

"Well… uh, if you really want it, I can arrange it." She was ready to duck.

Penny gave her an evil eye and sat down hard on the nearest chair.

"Fine, if that's what you want, but don't cry to me if you end all shook up."

"Penny, that's an Elvis song."

"Oh God, now I've got Elvis on my brain. Jim is off chasing Elvis killers and now you wanting Elvis to marry you and Blake. I need to go away for a while to clear my head."

"Why do you dislike Elvis?"

Penny sat quietly, then spoke, "Years ago, at my sweet sixteenth birthday party, no one showed up except an Elvis impersonator. He entertained me for almost two grueling hours as I waited for someone to show up. I was devastated and never forgave Elvis for ruining my big moment."

"But why did you blame Elvis for no one showing up?"

"My mother had put it on the invitations, I found out everyone just didn't want to see him. We were all young and the Beatles were the big thing back then, not Elvis. He was the old folk's singer. I just wanted someone to blame and he was handy. I've never told anyone that."

Val sat next to Penny and put her arm around her. "I'll never tell if you don't want me too."

"Just don't tell Jim, I don't want him going all gooey over my mental disaster. Thanks. Okay you can have Elvis preside at your wedding. I just hope people come to your ceremony."

"Penny, we have no one in this town to come, except you and Jim."

Penny realized this and said, "Oh no, not this time, I'm going to get all our friends to come, even if I have to threaten them. It will be a big occasion if I can help it. Now let's plan this wedding."

~~*~~

I was now frustrated. I had talked to about a dozen Elvi, plural, and barely got a straight answer from any of them, except the lawyer. Buck was having a great old time, Blake was wide-eyed over the strange assortment of odd balls. I'm not saying all Elvis impersonators are odd balls, just the ones I had to deal with. There were about a hundred more out in the convention center to deal with eventually. I can see why Lynn pawned this job off on me. I'd get her back.

I was getting cross-eyed with all the costumes, thankya's and hairdos. I looked to Blake and said, "What say we go see what the women are up to and see how much Penny has spent of my money."

Buck stood and said, "I'm going to stay around for a while and supervise my men, to make sure they know what to expect."

"Just tell them to watch out for a nut case carrying flammable liquids and a lighter. I'll call you later. Oh and where is Angelo?"

"He's still guarding the whiz kid at the electronic games convention over at the Vegas Convention Center."

Blue Suede Murders

"Maybe I'll take a swing by later to see how he's doing," I said and told Blake to follow.

Once out by the van, I pulled my cell phone and called Penny. She came on after a few rings, "Do you know who Val wants to do her wedding?" she yelled into the phone.

"Elvis. Blake already told me, I figured that would make you happy."

"Well she calmed me down and I gave in. Now we have to invite as many of our friends as possible to the wedding, I'm not letting Val have a lonely birthday party."

"Huh? What about a lonely birthday party?"

"Never mind, I didn't say that."

"Yes you did."

"I said I didn't say that, you hear me?"

"Yes dear." I knew better than to argue, I never won.

"Okay, now we have the dress, the reception and the Elvis minister, so Val is happy and I'm two-thirds happy."

"Where's the wedding going to be?"

"Same chapel as ours was, I think Shelby gets a kick back for using the place. But don't tell her that I said it. I have to go tie up a few loose ends. Talk later," she said and hung up.

I looked to Blake and said, "You poor fool you."

*

Chapter 8

Penny called back and said they were going to our home and we could meet them there. On the way I called Lynn, she came on after about six rings.

"Debating whether or not to answer my call?" I said.

"Something like that. You have any info for me?"

"Yes, arrest all the crazies at the MGM Grand and lock them up, if there's a killer amongst them, he or she will reveal themselves just to get away from all the nut cases. I'm still investigating, but after a full day of "Hound Dog" and "Heartbreak Hotel", I'm done for now. I need to talk to you about loose ends on this case, and about Troy Berlington. I think he is the key to the threats everyone else is getting."

"There's been more threats?"

"Yes, don't you even investigate anything?"

"I figured you were on the job," she said with a suppressed chuckle.

"Yes, I am and you will pay dearly for it." I hung up.

Blake was taking all this in and said, "Somethin' ah don't figure. How did the killer git all the Elvises phone numbers so he could call and threaten them?"

I about drove off the road. "Blake that's good detecting. I didn't even think about that. I guess I was so hung up on the idiots I dealt with I didn't look at the big picture. Thank you. I'll have to look into who has access to the personal information of all the performers and their phone numbers. It's a good lead."

Blake sat back being proud of himself. I glanced over and he was smiling widely. I had to hold in a laugh at his innocence. I hope marriage to Val and Vegas didn't corrupt him.

"You've never been married have you?" I asked.

"Nope, ah haven't. Ah jest never found the right woman. But now I have," he said with a puff of his chest.

"As a three times married man, I just want to say to be careful and do everything she says. Unless you can be firm and stand up to her. I don't really know Val that well other than her editing my books. I see a little of her personality in her recommendation on my stories, but I don't really know the real Val. You'll have to feel that out and go with it."

"Ah have seen her being vulnerable when she cried at night over bad times we went through out in Florida. She is very unsure of herself, but ah seem to bring out the best in her. She has told me that."

"Good, keep that up. It will help you to understand her and help her through the bad nights. Penny is a very strong person, I like that, she can take care of herself, which is good, but there are times I have to get her through the hard nights."

We pulled into my drive and I parked the van on the side. I got out and saw Angelo by the side of the guesthouse; I took Blake over to him.

"Angelo, this is my friend Blake. Blake this is Angelo, he works as a bodyguard for my firm. Speaking of bodyguarding, aren't you supposed to be watching some kid at a gamers convention."

"Pleasure to meet you Blake, I had been watching him but he was called back to Boston for some family business, and he didn't need me anymore. But they paid well for my short time with him."

"Good, we can always use it. Blake and I have been chasing down the Elvis killer."

"The one from the TV this morning?"

"Yes that one, it's been a long busy day. Do you have anything coming up for work now?"

Blue Suede Murders

"Lacey said there was some biggy movie star coming in and I may be on that tomorrow."

"Good, what are you doing out here?" I said when I saw he had a flat of plants on the ground and a trowel in his hand.

"Oh, I'm planting some fresh herbs, Mrs. R. said it would be alright. I use them for fixings in my dinners."

"Sounds good to me, have fun and I'll talk to you later." I led Blake to the front door of the house. I stopped and said to him, "Stay on that man's good side he is a useful person. He also is a retired mob figure and has connections."

Blake's eyes went big, "Mob, as in Mafia? Wow, how do you know him?"

"It's a long, long story, I'll tell it to you someday. Shall we go in and see what the women have in store for us?"

I opened the front door and Willy came barreling out of the kitchen and was jumping around Blake's feet. I just called him a traitor and went to find Penny and Val. They weren't in the kitchen and I called, but no answer. I was starting to worry a little and went out to the back. I found Penny and Val at the incinerator, which is what we called the huge adobe barbecue in our back yard. Val was tending some meat on the grill and Penny was sitting by watching.

"Hey Sweetie, you're home just in time, Val is a

whiz on the barbecue and is making us dinner. How was your day?'

"Lousy with Elvises. But that's another story for later. I am hungry, we haven't eaten all day now that I think on it. Smells great, I'll get the paper plates and dinnerware. Come with me Blake." I led him into the kitchen and we got out the stuff to eat off of, taking them back out to the picnic table. Penny went around the side of the house to the guesthouse and invited Angelo to join us. She had made sure there was enough food for everyone earlier.

We had our meal, Penny had made her trademark potato salad and it was all good. I was a little jealous that Val did such a good job on the barbecue as I was supposed to be the king of the grill. Blake was bragging on how great Val was at cooking. I could see the admiration in his eyes when he looked to her. It was good.

I turned to Angelo and asked, "How was it taking care of a kid?"

"It was okay, he was a little pain in the ass, but I kept him in check."

"You didn't break any of his legs did you?"

He laughed out loud and said, "Naw, but I did threaten him a couple times. I found a growl helped too."

Blake was in awe of Angelo, he sat watching the big man. I saw this and asked Angelo if he had a new job tomorrow.

"I got one to guard some Hollywood movie actor, I don't know who yet."

"What are they going to do?"

"There's some movie being made in Vegas and the actor's manager wants protection while they film. I just need to keep the fans and the paparazzi out of his hair."

"Blake how would like to follow Angelo around and help him?"

"Wow, could I?"

I looked to Angelo and said, "Blake is a cop from Florida, so he would be handy if there's trouble. I'll call Buck and tell him."

Val said, "Are you going to turn my Wubby into a bodyguard now?"

"Wubby? Come on Val, he's not a Wubby. He's a tiger, a fighting mongoose, he needs to see the real side of Vegas."

"If he gets hurt I'm coming after you," Val said with a grin.

"I carry a gun so be careful," I said.

We finished up and I said, "We should get the two of you into the honeymoon suite at the MGM Grand. I took a break earlier and left the convention to get you the room, it's all set. It's close to the room Penny and I had when we first came to Vegas during her convention for the talk show she got on nationwide TV. It has a great whirlpool."

Penny stood and then collected the clutter from the picnic table and dumped it all in the trash. I came up behind her and said, "You've been quiet for a while."

"I'm just tired, long day and Val was so energetic, she wore me down. I have enough steam to take them to the hotel but I'm going to bed early tonight."

"No problem for me, I had enough of the flying Elvises to last me. We'll both crash and get some sleep."

"Fine, that's why I love you," she said and kissed me.

Angelo went off to his guesthouse and we piled everyone into the van and drove to the motel were they had checked into and got their bags, then went to MGM Grand. I dropped the van at Valet parking and we went in to the front desk. I got the door card for their room and we went up. Once in the room Val was bouncing around loving the splendor of the place. Blake just stood with his mouth open looking around the big suite and I said to close his mouth, he did.

We begged off from visiting, leaving them to their own devices and back down to our van. We drove out to our humble home and I pulled into the drive and parked on the side.

Penny didn't move, I asked, "What's the matter?"

"I just got all happy helping Val get her wedding arranged. I'm sort of sad too."

"Why?"

"Well, I hope they will make it, they are both so young and most marriages end up falling apart. They hardly know each other, I'm worried they are rushing into it."

"They'll have to learn themselves. Not much you can do."

"We have a good marriage, don't we?"

"We do and I'm very happy with it, now shall we go in to bed?"

Penny looked to the bed in back of the van, she said, "I don't think I can make it into the house, meet you back there." She went to the back of the van and I followed.

*

Chapter 9

When we stumbled into the house in the morning we found that Angelo had already left. The note on the door said he'd wait for Blake at the office, so I had to roust him from his first night in the MGM Grand. I almost felt bad for him but I had a reason to get him involved with Angelo.

Penny was rushing to go to her job at the station and I got ready for the day chasing Elvises. Penny went off with Willy and I went to the van. I picked up Blake at the entrance to the MGM Grand, after he found his way down and got into the van.

"Where's Val?" I asked.

"Penny jest picked her up and they'all went off," he said with a smile.

"Good, Penny is quick in the morning, it worries me sometimes, but it's good."

We arrived at the agency and parked. I took Blake to meet Buck and he was in his office on the phone, looking officious. I had Blake sit and waited. Angelo came in and said good morning. He sat in another chair and gave me a big smile.

Buck finished, "So what's happening?"

"You're supposed to tell us that, you're the boss." I laughed and continued, "Buck, this is Blake Shelby, he's a police officer from Palatka, Florida."

"Oh yeah, he's the one you told me about involved in the serial killer case."

"Yes he is, and I want him to shadow Angelo on his bodyguarding job today."

"Okay, any reason for it?"

"Just let him go with Angelo, I'll explain it all later," I said.

"Okay, Angelo you got Blake to follow you, just don't let him kill anyone."

Angelo laughed and said, "I'll watch him and the client."

I patted Angelo on the back and bent down to say in his ear quietly, "Can I see you out in the hallway?"

I excused Angelo and me and we went out. "What's the deal Mr. R?" he said when we were out of earshot.

"Angelo, Blake is a really sweet, nice guy. I went through a week with him back in Florida and he did well chasing down a killer in the woods. But he's getting married sometime in the next week and I think he needs a little toughening up. I'm hoping that if he hangs with you for a day or two, you can rub off on him a little and he can man up a bit. Do you think you can help him without corrupting him?"

The big man laughed and said, "It would be a pleasure to teach him the life. I'll get him toughened up and ready for anything."

"Good man, I'll turn him over to you then," I said and we went back into the room.

"Okay Blake you are going with Angelo and I want you to play nice with him."

Blake grinned and said, "Ah'll do ma best."

Buck asked, "Blake, since you are a cop, do you carry?"

Blake grinned even wider and pulled his jean leg up revealing the service revolver strapped to his leg just inside his cowboy boot. "Ah never leave home without it."

"Good, you're all set, just don't shot any actors on the set."

Angelo took Blake out and I explained to Buck the method to my madness for having Blake follow Angelo around.

"Yep, being married needs some expertise in good old fashion mob leg breaking," Buck said.

"I have to go see Lynn and get some details from her on the Elvis killing. I hope it will be a lot saner than what we went through yesterday. How are your guards holding up?"

"I had two who wanted to quit and one who wanted to walk patrol through gangbanger land instead of watching the Elvises. They're not a happy bunch but they are doing the job."

"Okay keep me informed if anything strange goes on, I'll be at Metro." I went out to the lobby and Lacey had her head down to the file cabinets. I stood and then coughed slightly to warn her I was there, but she came up screaming a sharp yelp. "Damn it," she cursed.

I said sorry, I'm leaving and left the lobby quickly. I went to my van and drove out toward Metro headquarters. I called on my way in and Lynn said she was in her office. I went in and found Deacon standing in the back hallway reading a file.

"Hey Deacon, what's up?"

"Looking at a case of murder behind the Flamingo Hotel. Some hooker took a dumpster dive. Got no clues but her friends all say she had a date last night with a strip performer."

I remembered my old boss Nick North and his love of women that got him prison time. "Who's the headliner?"

"They aren't saying, claiming privilege, that's a laugh for hookers. We'll get him. How's it going with the Elvises?"

"Too damn many and too few intelligent answers. I'm needing info on Troy Berlington to see if it helps."

"You mean the charcoal briquette Elvis," he said with a smile.

"Yes Deacon, that Elvis. I'm going to see Lynn in her office."

"Yep, proceed with caution though; she's in a foul mood. It seems Weber is a really big fan of Elvis and he wants results fast."

"Good to know. Talk later." I went to Lynn's office and found her sitting back in her chair staring at the ceiling.

"Don't hurt yourself," I said from outside her door. She nearly went over backwards in her chair and yelped.

"Damn, Lacey said you were quiet when you sneak up on people," she said.

"I don't sneak, I'm just not noisy. Were you meditating?"

"I'm just pondering this Elvis burning. We don't have much, do you have anything?"

"A lot of weariness from talking to a couple dozen of the Elvi, plural. I get the impression that Troy was well liked in the community, but a lot of jealous impersonators weren't all that sad due to the murder."

"Well, from the street, I got nothing. There were no witnesses, and no surveillance camera caught anything coming from the alley where he was a hunka burning toast."

"I thought we couldn't do any song parodies?"

"You and Deacon can't, I can, I have the rank."

"Not over me, Deacon can cower in fear of you but I don't cower. Now what all do you have for me so far."

"Berlington worked the impersonator show at Harrahs and he was a draw for them. He finished his show after midnight and greeted his audience then went to his pink Cadillac, which he always parked with the Valet parking. They took care to see his car was parked safely. The valet on duty said he picked up the car just after one in the morning and he said he was taking a spin around the town before heading home. He pulled out and went north on the boulevard. The last anyone saw him."

"How did he end up in an alley off the strip?"

"Gee, I'll look into my crystal ball and pull up an answer for you," she said with frown.

"I was told you were touchy today."

"Who told you that? Deacon? I'm not touchy, I'm just under the gun to get this solved. Weber has a big thing for Elvis, I don't know how much, but he doesn't like the image of any Elvis being consumed in fire. He's making it personal goal to fix it and I'm the fixer."

"Okay, you're not touchy. A little grumpy maybe, but definitely not touchy."

"Better. Now CSI said he was doused with methyl ethyl ketone. A colorless flammable liquid used as a solvent for resins and as a paint remover for lacquers, adhesives and cleaning fluids. The perp hit him with a flame and he went up quickly. Poor bastard died quickly though according to Joe Lang. No witnesses were around to see."

"I've used methyl ethyl ketone and it is a nasty sweet-sickly smelling substance. I used it to clean brushes for a stain painting business I tried back in Michigan. There were no notes left anywhere to say why he was killed, no one is taking credit?"

"If you mean the We're-Sick-of-Elvis coalition, no, no note or statement. Just some disgruntled fan of either Elvis or Troy Berlington. Maybe you can track down some of his fans or lovers, it would help since you are in the trenches. I don't really want to go near an Elvis convention."

"I'll see what I can stir up because I 'Can't Help Falling In Love' with this case, so people won't be 'Crying in the Chapel' over a dead Elvis."

"You keep that up and they'll be crying over you. Please leave me to ponder some more."

I laughed and stood, "All right, I'll keep you informed." I left her office and nearly ran into Captain Weber.

Blue Suede Murders

"Richards, I hear you are helping to catch this despicable person who murdered our beloved Elvis."

"You do know he wasn't the real Elvis?"

"Of course I do, I'm not delusional, but he was a great Elvis, I saw his show many times, he could be the king." He walked off and I just stared after him.

Deacon came up and said, "That is one strange man. He has been mooning all morning over the death of this guy. It's amazing how much people worshiped Elvis. Enough to have a convention and impersonate him. This is all so bizarre."

"You're not telling me anything, I just spent about ten hours in Elvis hell and I'm ready to slit my wrists."

"Well, don't do it until you get Lynn something good. I can't live with her when she's in this mood."

"You have trouble living with her when she isn't, but I'll try," I said as I left the building.

*

Chapter 10

I drove back to the convention center at the MGM Grand and pulled the van into the parking structure. I was still very happy with the van, I could retire now and live in it, but I knew Penny would be objecting to that. We would be taking a good number of trips sightseeing around the west and central states when we could schedule the times and the small motorhome would be handy. Penny enjoyed the thing on our way back from the east coast after my book tour and she liked it because it was small and easy to keep clean.

I parked and went into the huge hotel and looked around the convention hall to find Morgan, he was with three impersonators, talking. I came up and stood behind them waiting, and listening.

"Freddy, for the first phase of the jumpsuit Elvis', you'll go on first followed by Ralph, George then when I find Charles Lawton, he'll go fourth. Good luck to all of you," he said and they finished their business. All walked off except Morgan who turned to see me.

"Mr. Richards, how are you this morning?" he said with a smile that looked more like an Elvis sneer. He did have an uncanny look of the younger Elvis around his movie days.

"I'm good, you're setting up the jumpsuit Elvis competition today?"

Blue Suede Murders

"Yes I am, it's just before the fat Elvis competition," he said and laughed hard. "Sorry, it's always been a joke to me when Elvis got so overweight and still tried to shake, rattle and roll. I would have thought with all the drugs he took back then, he would have slimmed down. Oh well, he was still the King."

"Yes, they say he was."

"You don't agree?"

"It's not so much agree or not, I just don't get the hero worship that people put on singers, like Sinatra or the Beatles."

"Well I have to agree with you. I only do this because I look a little like him and I found that he is a good business. I make a great deal of money shaking it on the stages for little old blue haired ladies who all worshipped the King back in the day. It takes people out of their mundane lives and gives them something to believe in. Hero worship? Yes it is and they eat it up."

"On another subject, do you have any thoughts on the murder of Troy Berlington?"

"That's a mystery to me, but Troy was the best and I think someone didn't like him being the best. Could it be a competitor, a rival, or a husband who didn't like him messing with his wife."

That caught my attention. "Was Troy a ladies' man? Could he have fooled around with the wrong woman?"

"I'd say it was a good bet. Troy was, as you say, a ladies' man. He had them coming and going and wasn't ashamed to be seen with the wrong women. I'm actually surprised he lasted this long."

"So you do have an idea for a motive. Any one woman in particular or did he have a number of angry women pining over him?"

"Oh he had the women pining all right. Troy would spot one woman in the audience and concentrate on her. He didn't care who she was with because he knew she would be with him at the end of the night. I've heard stories of his all night orgies that would curl your hair." He looked up to my baldhead and said, "Sorry that was a figure of speech."

"No offense taken, my hair has been curled a good number of times. I like the joke about it rubbing too many bed headboards."

Morgan laughed and then, "If you want to look into anyone, there's one performer who may have cause to do in Troy, he was one of the Rat Pack impersonators, the Dean Martin performer. Not the regular one, but the guy who would come in to fill for the regular guy in the show. He was one of the performers who went on tour across the country with the Rat Pack touring show. He's been in town because the regular Deano has been on vacation."

"What's this guy's name?"

"Max Petrocelli, he's another ladies' man but he's married to a blond bimbo who Troy has been tapping for a while, when Max was out of town on tour. Convenient set-up for Troy, or was. If you need a place to start, I'd say he's a good bet."

"Do you have any opinion of Max, is he violent?"

"I heard he broke up a hotel room at the Tropicana one night after he caught his wife with a minor headliner. The headliner got out of the room before Max got hold of him, but Max was hauled in for destruction of private property."

"Who was the headliner, may I ask?"

He grinned and said, "I hear you worked at one time for Nick North? Maybe he might have been the guy."

I laughed, "Yes, Nick was a whore hound, but he's cooling in prison now. I'm sure he's not dating the right sex there."

Morgan laughed and said, "I have to go get this circus started, talk later?"

"Sure, you seem to have a good knowledge of Vegas scandals. I'd like to talk more."

He started to go then turned, "I understand that a few of our performers are going to be on your wife's show this afternoon. I think your wife is a very good host, I also understand the she's not too crazy about Elvis, so it should be interesting." He smiled and went off.

I suddenly had a dread run through me. Penny hadn't mentioned Elvis being on her show, and she would have been ranting about it. So that meant she didn't know yet. I could feel the earth shake, the buildings around me falling over and crashing to the ground as MegaPenny tore through Vegas tearing at the seams of the city. The army would send out jets with warheads to bring her down. She would finally go off to Lake Mead and disappear into the depths of the lake, only to be seen occasionally as the monster of lake. My cell phone rang and I looked to the caller ID, it was Penny. I was frightened.

"Are you holding up babe?" I said as I answered.

"You knew about this didn't you?"

"No dear, I just found out about two minutes ago, I was going to call and warn you to run, but I guess you know now."

"I'm going to be so glad when this week is over and I never have to put up with Elvis again. I am still looking for Gordy, the coward is hiding in the studio somewhere. I'll find him, he set this up without consulting me. I will find him." She hung up. I was hoping Gordy, Penny's producer, made it out of the studio safely. I really need to know why Penny hated Elvis so much. I'd have to really bug her to tell me one day when she was good and drunk.

Blue Suede Murders

I turned back to the auditorium as the people were filing in to watch the jumpsuit competition. I had to chuckle thinking that if this were a beauty pageant, they'd be having the swimsuit competition right now instead of the jumpsuit. I'd rather see the swimsuits, but not on the Elvises.

I took a seat behind the judges again and Nolan Clark was back on the panel. I was wondering if they had asked Penny if she'd like to judge but figured they knew of her opinion about Elvis. Nolan turned to look back at the crowd and saw me.

"Hey Jim, you must be really enjoy this?"

"I'm working, the flaming Elvis case."

"Ah, I see. I'm the last one to know."

"But you work for the local newspaper. Don't you keep informed?"

"Hell, I write gossip, I don't pay attention to facts," he laughed and turned back to the stage.

I endured the show, it wasn't actually bad. The first three impersonators had done their thing, shaking it on the stage. It was Charles Lawton's turn and I was waiting along with everyone else for Morgan to announce him, then the lights went dim and a spotlight hit stage center. There was Charles in his best Elvis pose. The music cranked up to "Suspicious Minds" causing a stir in the crowd. They were on their feet as Charles went into the gyrations and deep knee bends. I was amazed that he had a hold on the crowd, but he looked and acted just like Elvis. These fans probably never saw the real Elvis, so this was something that brought them close to the original show.

Lawton was just into the final phase of the song when he suddenly stopped, looking shocked and collapsed to the stage. I stood wondering what was happening as Morgan and someone I presumed was the stage manager ran out to him. They hovered over him for a couple seconds as they checked him, then Morgan stood and said something to the stage manager. He ran off the stage and the curtain closed.

I went to the steps going up to the stage and in behind the curtain. I saw a number of people standing around Lawton on the floor. I came up to Morgan who was looking very pale now.

"Morgan, what happened?" I asked.

He looked to me, "You have your work cut out for you, he's dead, shot in the head."

*

Chapter 11

I immediately went back to the curtain, finding the opening and went through. I stood on the stage; the lights were up in the auditorium and I looked around trying to see where a shooter would hide. There was a balcony high up and the shot could have come from there, but the killer would have to be one hell of a shot to hit Charles from that distance.

Morgan came through the curtain also; he had a wireless microphone and announced that Charles was ill and that the show would continue shortly.

I went off the side of the stage still looking out and realizing that I was exposed to whoever wanted to kill people, but I figured the killer hit the person he or she wanted, so I should be safe. I hoped. I couldn't see anyone, but that was the point, not to be seen. I heard no gunshot, so either the killer had a silencer or the music was loud enough to cover the sound.

I went back to where Charles was and looked down to him. He had blood coming from a small hole in his temple, suggesting that he was standing sideways when he was shot, or the killer was off the side of the auditorium. I wondered if anyone had videotaped the show. I'd have to ask.

Morgan came back to me and said he had called the police. I wondered if Lynn and Deacon would be in shortly, I waited. A few minutes later Morgan had the judge's results in front of the closed curtain covering the crime scene. Morgan told the judges to disregard Charles' performance, but didn't explain. The prize went to some guy named Frank Lane and he accepted his trophy happily. I wondered about him, he was off the side of the stage when the shot was fired. Could he have done it? I really was hating Elvises now.

Lynn and Deacon came storming in and had a whole swarm of cops with them. The auditorium was closed and no one was allowed to leave. Lynn gave me a look, went to the stage front and announced that there had been a shooting and everyone was to stay in his or her seats until the police could talk to them. I knew this would probably start a riot but waited.

Lynn came to me, "You were here when this happened, who did it?"

"You think I really know, thank you for the vote of confidence, but I couldn't see where he was shot from. I'll check my crystal ball," I joked.

"Smart ass. Do you have anything for me?"

"Yes, you have an auditorium full of crazy Elvis fans out there waiting to go have a good time, you have your work cut out for you."

Lynn just sighed and yelled for Warren, who came running, "Greg, go start the interrogation of the fans and take Williams with you." He ran off and Lynn turned to me, "Please help me with this. When Weber heard we had another Elvis death, I could hear him yelling from his office. I just ran out the back to avoid him and I'm sending his calls to voice mail."

"He's not going to like that," I said.

"I know, but I have nothing but two dead Elvises now, and I'm no further than I was two days ago."

"I may have a lead for you, if you want to check up on it." I paused.

"What?"

"Okay, there was a woman's husband who may have been troubled by Troy's dalliances with his wife."

"But what about this guy?"

"Hmm... That's something we need to dig into. I don't know if he was involved with the wife."

"Okay so you have nothing. Thanks."

"Hey, it's only been two days. I'm not a TV crime fighter. This crime doesn't get solved in an hour."

My cell phone buzzed and I saw it was Penny, "Excuse me while I go listen to my wife yell while you go talk to about five hundred people." I smiled and walked to the side of the stage. "Hello."

"I'm calming down now, I'm accepting this but I still want to strangle someone, but I'll let it pass. Hi Sweetie, how's your day going?"

"Well, I have another dead Elvis, otherwise the day is going nicely."

"What! Another dead Elvis, what is going on? I thought I was the only person who hated Elvis, I have a competitor?"

"Well, since you put it that way, yes you do. Lynn and Deacon are here trying to look official. I'm not any further ahead than this morning, so it's all good. Is Val having a good time?"

"She's loving all the Elvises, and I have her taking care of Willy, keeping her busy. I had to talk to the Elvises, one to one. It was something I wasn't ready for. I got through it, you would be proud of me."

"I am, are the Elvises gone now?"

"Bet your sweet bippy they are. My studio is back to normal. Elvis has left the building. So what are you going to do now?"

"I'm going to try and find a killer in about five hundred people, wish me luck."

"Wish! And I'll see you later, oh are you bringing Blake with you or dropping him off at the MGM?"

"I don't know, what are you going to do with Val? Why don't you take her to the house and we'll meet you there."

"It's a plan. See you later." She hung up and I put my cell away. I turned to see Lynn talking to Morgan while Deacon was downstage watching Joe Lang examine the body. I went to Deacon, it was probably safer.

"Jim, can't you watch these guys better? I thought you were supposed to have bodyguards on them."

"Well, we can't guard a person when he has to stand in front of five hundred possible Elvis assassins. Off stage it's a different matter. Our man was nearby for when he finished. We just didn't think it would happen while he was bouncing around the stage."

"Well this is now bordering on serial killing. I hope we don't get more."

"I don't have enough men to protect everyone, and short of shutting down the convention, we don't have much to stop another."

"Hey if we stop the convention, everyone would go home and Vegas would be back to normal."

"There are still a lot of Elvises living here you know. The killer doesn't discriminate, Berlington was a resident, although our latest body lived in LA. He came here and worked here enough to qualify as a resident."

"Okay, so far only local performers were murdered," Deacon said thoughtfully.

"Yes, so it may be a local who wants either to be the top Elvis here or a local resident who is out to get rid of Elvis."

"I like the competitor angle," Deacon said.

"What competitor angle?" Lynn asked as she came up behind us.

"We're just theorizing on who the killer could be, a competitor or a local civilian who hated Elvis," I said.

"Don't forget Penny, does she have an alibi?" Lynn said with a smile.

"Yes, she called me from her studio and has witnesses. So she's ruled out."

"Okay Mr. Eye-spy, what happened here from your point of view?"

"I was sitting behind the judges while Lawton was doing his act, I saw him looking shocked and he went down. I didn't see him get hit, it was fast and clean. I didn't hear a shot, but the music was loud and may have covered the noise. Morgan, who you just met, and one of the stage people came out and then they closed the curtains. I went up and then looked out to the audience but could see nothing. The balcony is just too far for that good of a hit. I'm thinking it came from the wings of the stage. There are catwalks up for the rigging, maybe it came from there, and the noise would have been covered by the thick curtains."

"Okay, I'll buy that." She looked to Deacon and said, "Let's gather everyone who was backstage and start questioning them." She turned and went to Morgan again and said something to him. He yelled to the same man who came out front with him, the stage manager I presumed, and they started to gather people from the back stage area.

About a half hour later, most of the audience was cleared out by the patrol cops who came in to help question people. There were about fifteen people on stage waiting to be questioned, and then Lynn had them all come off the stage and sit in the first row of auditorium seats. The place was cleared by Lynn's men searching for evidence of the shooting in the auditorium and balcony; they found nothing. Joe Lang had carted off Lawton's body but not before he expressed his disapproval of the Elvis killings.

"This is not good for Vegas or the great performers who keep Elvis alive," Joe said.

I asked, "Joe, have you ever seen the real Elvis?"

"I did when I was younger. My mother would bring me to the hotel showrooms where he would work around town, it was magical. This is so sad." He went off when he was called by an assistant.

I looked to Lynn and said, "Maybe these Elvises were murdered because someone thought they were mocking the King? A disgruntled fan of the real Elvis?"

"I hope you're not trying to pin this on Joe?"

"Do you really know Joe?"

Lynn smiled and said, "You don't know Jack." Then she laughed and walked away.

*

Chapter 12

I called Angelo to see how they were holding up and he answered after the second ring. "Mr. R. what's up?" he said.

"Just calling to see if all is well in movie land."

"It okay, just boring as hell. Waiting around for the director ta get a good take. Blake is getting restless. I've been talking ta him and I think I might be getting through. He's a good kid, I like him. I hope his wedding goes well."

"I intend to see that it does, I'm hoping a day or two with you will get him to become a little tougher, when do you think you will be done at the shoot?"

"The director is about done with my client, about an hour they say. I then take him back to his hotel and get him safely past the paparazzi and into his room. Then we can leave. I figure two hours tops. I'll call you when we finish."

"Good Angelo, I'll wait for you then. Talk later," I said and hung up.

One job taken care of, hopefully Blake will start being a little less shy. I'm sure Blake and Val are good in the sex department, I just wanted him to be a little more assertive in everyday things. Maybe Val was the dominate one in their relationship. Maybe I was rocking the boat. I'll worry about it later.

I looked around for either Lynn or Deacon, but they were nowhere to be seen. I went back on to the stage and looked up around at the catwalk from where someone could have used a gun. The stage crew usually has a man up there to control the curtains and fly-ins, he would have seen someone if there was a person up there who shouldn't be. The union crew takes a dim view on intruders in their areas.

I heard noises behind me and turned to see Lynn and Deacon coming up to the people sitting in the front row waiting to be questioned. I walked to the stairs going down to the main floor and went to sit on a chair by the person on the end. Lynn was now speaking.

"Everyone who was on the back of the stage when Lawton was killed, please think of who was standing near you. Look around at all the people seated here for that person and if you don't see them let me know now."

Everyone was straining to see the other people seated on the chairs, then one man spoke. "I don't see the Elvis who was watching from the back. He wasn't a contestant but told me he was just watching. I didn't care if he did or not, it wasn't my business, so I let him watch."

"And you are?" Lynn asked.

"I'm Jimmy, the head electrician, I take care of the mics and sound system from the back stage."

"Could you remember this man well enough to recognize him again?"

"No offense detective; but these Elvises all look alike to me. He had no discernable features, he was kind of feminine looking actually, but unremarkable. I might, just might be able to spot him, but I doubt it. He had on the early Elvis, leather and jeans. Now that I think of it, his hair was a bit done up too much. Almost a goofy caricature of Elvis."

"Did anyone else see this person?"

No reply. "Okay, everyone please give your names and contact number to the officer I will send to you and then you can go." Lynn went to a uniform and said something to him; he nodded and went to gather the information. She came over and sat in the chair next to me.

"I hope we can get something from the two videos we got from the people in the audience who were taping the thing. Luckily, my officers had asked people if they were taping and found ones who made videos of the show. CSI can run it and get a fix on where the shooter was standing."

Deacon came up with a man carrying a video camera. "I found this guy who sat in the center, third row back and he recorded the hit. We can watch it."

Blue Suede Murders

We all went to the stage and the man put the Sony Handicam on the platform and started it. We tried to look at the small screen jutting out from the camera, watching Lawton doing his thing and then we could see his head jerk slightly and he looked surprised. He was facing directly out to the audience so the hit had to come from off the side. Lynn said the same as I thought.

I looked up to the stage and tried to visualize the scene I saw in the video and the shot had to have come from between two curtains that were hanging on the side of the stage, less than twenty feet from where Lawton was. It would be a good hiding place. I went up the stairs and over to the curtains and separated them. Lynn came up behind me as I bent down to see a shell casing on the floor.

Lynn pulled a rubber glove hanging from her back pocket and picked up the shell. "Twenty-two, just like Joe said hit him in the head. I'll pass this to CSI and see if we get lucky for a print, but I doubt it." She went off and I stayed looking around the curtain, just as Lynn yelled back to get away from the area until CSI could sweep the scene. I carefully walked away not wanting to leave any evidence of my own.

I spent another hour watching the dissemination of the crime scene and Lynn was huffing around trying to get everyone to find something to give her a lead. I knew I had nothing else to go on for now, I wanted to check on the other woman lead I had, but would do that tomorrow.

Thankfully, my cell phone buzzed and it was Angelo. "Hello."

"Mr. R. we're finished for the day. Just leaving the hotel where I put the client in his room. Where do you want to meet?"

"Go to the office, I'll meet you there." I hung up and told Lynn I was leaving. She just waved me off and went back to yelling at her people. Poor woman, I did have sympathy for her knowing Weber was in a rush to get the crime solved. I went out to the van and drove over to the office.

I parked in back and went in to find Angelo and Blake standing in the inner lobby talking to Lacey.

Lacey saw me and said, "I'm not talking to you."

"That's a welcome relief. Okay I give, can you talk long enough to say why?" I said.

"You didn't invite me to go see the Elvises perform. You took Blake and didn't even ask me."

"I didn't know you liked Elvis and I'm working a case not conducting a field trip. Besides, if you went who would run the office?"

"Tracey can handle the walk-ins and paperwork can get done in time. So I need to go next time."

"Well there was another Elvis murdered today, as I sat watching, shot in the head. I don't want you to get caught in the crossfire if it happens again."

Blue Suede Murders

"Another! This is not good. I need to go and I'll need to take a weapon!"

"No Lacey, you have the gun in your desk for office protection use only. It's not to be carried out of this building. You hear me?"

"Well I still want to go."

I paused and she seemed determined to go, "All right, I'll take you but just to watch the competitions, nothing more and you will sit away from the stage so you don't get hit by a stray bullet, you hear?"

"Goody, when do we go?"

"Tomorrow, they have more competitions going then. There probably will be police scouring the auditorium for sharpshooters, so it will be a circus. And the morbid people will want to be there to see if someone else gets killed."

"I'll be ready," she said with a big grin. I was going to regret it, but if I didn't take her I would also regret it. So either way I lose.

I turned to Angelo and Blake and said, "Let's go into my office."

We were seated and I asked the men if they'd like a drink as I reached to my fridge and pulled out a beer. I had a small liquor cabinet put in the room on top of the fridge and it had the basics, scotch, bourbon, Johnny Walker Red and Black, rum, well all the good stuff. I had it for occasions that called for a drink.

"Angelo, name your poison."

"JW Red, neat."

"Blake?"

"Well if'n you'all don't mind, do ya have a Pepsi?"

"I do, but this occasion calls for something stiffer." I pulled out the whiskey and poured a generous amount into the large glasses in the cabinet and handed each their drinks. I held up my beer and said "Down the hatch."

Blake took a good swig but not all, and just about choked on it. He was sputtering as Angelo and I tried not to laugh.

"Wow, that's hot going down."

"Have you ever had whiskey before?" I asked.

"No sir, that whar ma first. It is making ma head tingle. Whoo!"

"Okay, let's bottoms up."

Angelo drank his drink down and Blake saw him, so he tipped his up and swallowed it all. I was waiting for his eyes to settle from crossing, then he just sat smiling.

"Ah, not bad," was all he said, then put his head back and passed out.

Chapter 13

"You did what?" Penny yelled as Angelo carried Blake into our living room. He gently put Blake down on the couch and said quietly to me, "I'm going to my room now before Mrs. R. tears you a new one." He went off as I was left standing there feeling like a boy who shot the pet cat.

"We were celebrating Blake's pending marriage; I didn't know he couldn't hold his liquor."

"You're lucky Val is out swimming. We have to wake him before she..."

"What's going on?" Val asked as she came into the room, wrapped in a towel. She stopped short when she saw Blake on the couch passed out. "Oh no, is he dead?"

"No he's just passed out. He'll live."

"What happened?"

"We were having a celebratory drink and it seems he can't hold his liquor," I said hoping Blake would wake up soon.

Val went to him, "Wubby! Wake up. Wubby! He's dead isn't he?" she said as she looked up to me.

"Val take it easy, he's just passed out."

"Oh God, we didn't even make it to the altar. Poor Wubby baby."

"Val, he's not dead. He'll wake up soon with a small headache. But he will wake." I looked to Penny, "He only had one drink, then he went belly up. I've never seen anyone pass out from one drink."

"Wubby, come back to me. Come back from the other side." Val was in tears now, I was a dead man myself when Penny got hold of me. Maybe Angelo and I should have sobered him up first.

Blake suddenly opened his eyes and then sat up with Val's help. "Where am ah?"

"Wubby, you are all right. Oh I'm so happy."

"Val, how did ah get here?"

She looked to me with squinty eyes; I just stepped back behind Penny. She pushed me away and said, "Don't hide behind me, you murderer."

"He isn't dead, he's fine, and I'm not a murderer." I defended.

"Wow, that drink was strong!" Blake said. "Ah don't think ah could do that agin."

He was wobbling on the couch, I said, "See, he's going to be fine. Now he just needs to walk it off that's all."

Blue Suede Murders

Val and I helped Blake up and he wobbled more as she took him to the back of the house and out the door to the backyard. He held his hand up over his eyes from the sun and made a puppy noise. "That hurts."

Penny gave me a face, "What, it's not the end of the world," I defended.

She stopped me and said, "Blake is a sweet boy and you better not corrupt him, you hear?"

"Yes dear." It was all I could say.

About an hour later, Blake and Val were sitting on the picnic table as I grilled some steaks, hoping it would make up for nearly killing Blake. According to Penny.

We ate as Blake was relating his day at the movie shoot. Val was pouring herself over him, hanging on to his every word. I was glad she was so devoted to him, after her experience with the serial killer in Florida, she needed someone to take care of her. My little boy was growing up.

We finished our picnic and Val said she wanted to go back to the hotel to rest, it was a long day. When Blake and I were alone, I asked him if he was all right, he smiled and said he was.

"Ah think this was a milestone day for me. Mah first real drink and I git to see genuine movie stars. It has been good."

"I'm glad. Now do you still feel like following Angelo tomorrow?"

"Ah shore do, It's good for me to see how the other side lives. Ah need to live a little."

"Well, I hope you have a good time and I'll remember not to give you any alcohol again."

"Don't fret about it, ah never drank when I was young, it jest hit me wrong. Plus ah didn't have anything to eat before that."

"Yeah, that will do it. Okay we'll drive you and Val back to the MGM and you can sleep it off."

Val was still fretting over Blake and then we drove them back to the hotel and dropped them off. On the way back to our home, Penny broke out in laughter.

"What's wrong with you?" I asked.

"I'm not dumb, even if I act like it at times. I knew what you were doing, putting Blake in situations that would toughen him up."

"How did you know that?"

"First, Angelo and I talk in the mornings and second, you talk in your sleep."

"I do not!"

"Yes you do, especially after a few beers, you just pour your soul out to me. You told me all about your plan to help Blake grow up a little. I think that's very nice of you, that boy does need to grow up."

"Boy? Hell, he's thirty-one and hasn't even had a drink in his life. I can't let him go into marriage with that behind him. I would think these country boys were experienced in life early on. I didn't even have my first drink until I was nineteen. And I was behind the other guys in my social circle."

"Well, it's good. I arranged for Val and Blake's wedding to be a week from tomorrow, in the afternoon. I need to call around and get as many people to come as possible. You do the same with your friends."

"All my friends are your friends. But I think I can come up with a few that you don't know. Why the big concern for this to be a big wedding. I can understand the fact they don't know anyone out here, but you seem obsessed with this being a big occasion."

"I just want them to have a nice wedding," she said.

"Okay I understand that, and have you accepted Elvis to perform the ceremony."

"Reluctantly, yes."

"Why do you have such a dislike for Elvis?"

She was silent for a while, I didn't push it, just waited.

"When I was born, I was delivered by an Elvis impersonator, he sang "Happy, Happy Birthday, Baby" then segued into "The First Time Ever I Saw Your Face" and "Got A Lot O' Living to Do". He struck a pose and slapped my ass. I've never been able to watch an Elvis again."

I wasn't going to challenge that, I just smiled and drove home in silence. Penny was watching out the window, grinning.

It was Saturday morning and we were still in bed when I heard the driveway alarm go off. "Crap, I didn't want to get up yet," I said to Penny who had her head under the pillow.

I got up and stumbled to the front door when I heard the bell ring. I peeked out the peephole and was greeted by Will Trapper's smiling face.

"What are you doing here so early?" I asked as I opened the door to let him in.

"I heard you are investigating the Elvis convention and I want to go with you."

"I didn't know you are a fan of Elvis?'

"Oh yeah, I'm a hunka-hunka burning fan of his. Sorry I wasn't around when you first took on the case. What do you have so far?"

I took him to the snack bar and had him sit while I started coffee for him. Penny came out in her robe looking still half-asleep. She saw Will and said good morning, turned and went back to the bedroom.

I told him all the details of the case as he sat sipping the coffee and making faces.

"If you don't like my coffee, next time bring your own. Now I have to get dressed and if you want to tag along at the Elvis convention, it's good with me." I left him and went back to the bedroom and didn't see Penny. I heard water running from her bathroom and figured she was showering. I went to my bathroom and got ready.

I came out and found Penny all dressed and ready to go. It still amazed me how she can go from the living dead to fully awake and eager to go.

"So what's the agenda for the convention this morning? I'm going with you."

"You want to go into a building full of Elvises?"

"Val will be with me, so I'll be safe. She's one tough broad like me. The Elvises won't stand a chance."

I didn't like what I was hearing, but again, it was useless to argue with her. I hated to admit when it came to her, I was a wimp.

"Okay, you and Val can go but I have to do something first." I had finished dressing and went out to my home office and called Angelo. "Angelo, it's me. Change of plans. I need Blake today so go ahead to your job and we'll talk later." He agreed and hung up. I called Blake and said, "Blake, it's Jim. I need you today for another task. It's very dangerous and you may not come back alive."

I could hear him laugh and he said, "Ah know, ah'm escorting Val and Penny to the Elvis convention. Val already tole me."

Great, they plot things without telling me. This world is being taken over by women. "Okay, we'll be by in a little while to pick you up. I'll call when we get there." We finished and I hung up.

I said to myself, "I have a feeling this is going to be one very strange day."

*

Chapter 14

I was driving Penny and Trapper to stop by the office to pick up Lacey then the MGM Grand to go to work hunting the Elvis killer, gather Val and Blake, and to turn them loose to go explore the Elvis convention with Penny. I was still amazed that Penny wanted to go, but it was a breakthrough.

"What's in the bag by your seat?" Penny asked looking down at the bag with the Elvis t-shirt I bought the other day for Penny as a joke.

She reached down and picked it up, looked inside and pulled out the shirt. She studied it for a moment as I said, "I got it for you, okay, it was a gag gift."

Blue Suede Murders

"You got this as a gag gift for me?"

"That's what I said."

Trapper spoke from the passenger chair behind me, "Knowing Penny's dislike for Elvis, that was a cruel gift to get her."

"Did anyone ask you?" I said.

He shut up. Penny just smiled, "Since this was a gag gift I can do anything I want with it, right? Right?"

"Yes, dear, anything you want, but just don't throw it away. It wasn't cheap."

"Well, I'm honored you thought enough of me to spend money. Thank you."

She folded the shirt, put it back in the bag and held it on her lap. We arrived at the MGM Grand and I parked in the structure next to the hotel and we went in to find Val and Blake. They were waiting by the convention hall doors and waved when they saw us.

I saw Morgan standing by the registration table and excused myself from my friends and wife. "Morgan, I have a small request. My wife and our friends would like to watch the competitions. Would they be able to slip in to watch?"

"No problem Jim, let me get some badges for them to go to the rest of the convention also." He picked up five badges and handed them to me, "Just have them wear these and they can go visit all of the convention."

"Thanks that's very nice of you, appreciate it."

"Any word on Lawton's death yesterday?"

"None yet, I have to talk to Lynn Carter to see what forensics came up with, I'll let you know."

He thanked me and I went back to where I left my little band of Elvis lovers. I stopped just before getting there when I saw that Blake was wearing the Elvis t-shirt. He looked uncomfortable but Val was beaming and was smoothing the shirt on him. Penny gave me her evil grin as I came up and handed out the badges.

"Wear these for anywhere in the convention. Call on your cell phone when you are bored of all this. Nice shirt Blake, you're a hunka-hunka burning love now." He just looked more uncomfortable and tried to smile.

Val came to me and pulled me away from the others. "Jim I want to ask you a big favor?"

"Name it."

"Would you give me away at the wedding?"

"I'd be honored to Val, thank you for asking."

She gave me a kiss on the cheek and we went back to the group.

Blue Suede Murders

I looked to Trapper and said, "Do you want to follow them to ogle Elvis, or go investigate with me?"

"I'll follow you; you get to go to good places others can't go."

"Fine, now everyone remember where we parked." I made the joke in reference to a Star Trek movie I once saw and then took Trapper's arm and pulled him away from the rest.

We went back to Morgan and I introduced Trapper to him. "Morgan, this is my partner in crime fighting, Will Trapper. I brought him in to help. Will, this is Morgan Taylor, head Elvis."

"Good to meet you Morgan," Trapper said and shook hands.

"What is on the agenda for today?" I asked.

"More performers to narrow down for the big prize, today is the older in life Elvises, as I said, the fat ones." He laughed at this joke and continued, "I noticed that there are a number of police in the auditorium and backstage. I feel safer all ready."

"Is Lynn Carter here now?"

"She's backstage doing her cop business."

"Thanks, we'll go visit her," I said and led Trapper into the auditorium. We went up the side door to the backstage area where I saw Lynn and Deacon talking to three uniforms. She turned her head and saw me, she waved and then the cops left her.

"Will, are you slumming with this cheap version of Mike Hammer?"

Trapper laughed and said, "I had nothing better to do."

"So you have the place being watched closely now," I said.

"Yep, if anyone even tries anything we got everyone covered."

"Great, when does the show begin?"

"About an hour, we're frisking anyone backstage now. Do we have to pat you down?"

"No thanks, I think Will and I can just go look the convention over and well be back."

"Ok, sit in front so you can see anything we may miss."

"Shall do." I took Trapper back out the stage door and into the big hall where there were booths set up to hawk Elvis products and promote various impersonators. This part of the convention was open to the public and it was nearly packed. Trapper and I walked around as I explained a few more details about the case.

We turned a corner and I stopped. Trapper hit his brakes and asked what was wrong.

Blue Suede Murders

I pulled him to the side of a booth and said, "Very carefully look over to the booth with the Flying Elvises para-sail team."

Trapper looked around the corner of the booth we were hiding behind and stared. "I don't see anything."

I came up next to him, pointed to three Elvises all talking to each other and said, "Who does the middle Elvis look like?"

Trapper was studying the man then he suddenly made a guttural noise and said, "Weber!"

"Exactly what I thought. He's dressed like jumpsuit Elvis complete with big hair. This is precious. Shall we go say hi?" I asked.

"No! I have a better idea." He reached into his jacket pocket and came out with his Minolta point and shoot camera that he always carried. He brought it up, zoomed in and snapped a bunch of pictures of Captain Weber. "This is going on the precinct's computers as a backdrop. I love it. Let's get out of here before he sees us."

We went around the booth and explored the arena a bit more before going back to the auditorium.

I saw Penny and her followers sitting in the fourth row on the end and she saw me, waved and then I saw Morgan walking toward her. I was wondering what he was asking her and I saw her shake her head, then Morgan said something else and she was still, then stood. Morgan led her to the judge's table and had her sit in a vacant seat. I was a bit stunned.

I went to the table saying hi to Nolan Clark and went to Penny. "What are you doing?"

"I'm a celebrity, I was asked to fill in for a sick judge. Isn't this a riot?"

"But can you be objective, since you hate Elvis?'

"Hate is such a strong word, detest is much better, but I can judge on performance and imitation."

Nolan leaned over and laughed, "Yeah Jim, it's not rocket science to pick a good Elvis from the others."

"Who pulled your chain?" I asked with a smile. "Babe, just don't make any statements before you pick a winner."

Morgan was on stage announcing the start of the show. I took Trapper back to where Val, Blake and Lacey were and we sat.

I was hoping our Elvis killer didn't want to get rid of the judges. I was still puzzled by why someone would want to kill Elvis? I needed to follow up on the love triangle angle. Triangle angle? That's a funny phrase. I was amusing myself when the lights went down and the show began.

Morgan welcomed the fans and then introduced the judges. He came to Penny and gave her profile as a talk show host of Vegas Alive in the morning and former national talk show host. Penny stood and waved to the crowd when Morgan asked her to. I was thinking she shouldn't make a target out of herself, then she sat back down.

The show went on without a hitch or death. Lynn's cops were patrolling the place and it would be difficult for anyone to do anything criminal.

Trapper spoke, "That was disappointing. Not that I wanted anyone killed but that was boring. None of these guys impressed me. Lousy impersonations."

I smiled as Morgan gathered the sheets from the judges, wondering how Penny managed to get through it. Morgan went back up to the stage as all the Elvises waited for the verdict.

He finally announced the winner and they gave out the small trophies to the runners-up. Penny was smiling and I was proud of my girl for making it to the end without breaking down. The competition ended and she stood shaking Nolan's hand and came over to us.

"Well, that was good of you," I said.

She gave me a look and said, "What?"

"I said you did good."

She stared and then said, "Oh, hold on." She reached up and pulled earplugs out of her ears and put them in her purse.

"You had earplugs in?"

"Yep, Nolan Clark gave them to me to get through the show. I just judged on their performance. I didn't really want to hear them."

I was amazed.

*

Chapter 15

Penny, Val, Blake and Lacey went off to explore all the Elvis goodies, while Trapper and I went to find Lynn and Deacon. We wound our way through all the fans and impersonators in the auditorium. I couldn't see them in the huge room but then they came out of the stage door and saw me.

They came up and Lynn said, "Well, there was no attempt on the Elvises this time. Probably because there were way too many cops around. You have anything that you may have seen out here?" Lynn asked.

"No, nothing other than a lot of Elvis fans all bouncing around and screaming. I'm going take Trapper and go to question a woman who had an affair behind her husband's back with Berlington and finding out if she knew Lawton. Unless you have a better lead?"

"No, go chase fallen women, but keep me informed."

"Oh wait," Trapper spoke and pulled out his camera, "You may be interested in this." He turned on the camera, brought up the previews and showed them Weber in uniform. Lynn and Deacon busted a gut laughing and said to email them the pictures. She gave Trapper her business card with her email address.

I said we had to go and took Trapper out of the auditorium. I called Penny and said we were leaving for a while and would be back later. Penny said that was all right, they would go explore the strip after they were done here. I said I'd call when we got back.

Yesterday, I had asked Morgan about the mystery woman involved with Berlington and he provided the name. I got the info on her location from Warren when I called him earlier before leaving my home since I didn't want to bother Lynn.

We drove up to an apartment complex off Maryland Avenue, pulled into the lot and sat for a moment gathering our thoughts.

"Do you think this woman could be the key to the murders?" Trapper asked.

"She could be for Berlington, he had an affair with her and she is married. The husband may have found out and torched Berlington. I just don't know what the connection to Lawton is yet. If she was fooling around with him the hubby may have figured that since he murdered once why not twice."

"It makes sense to me, how you going to play it?"

"Well, we could try the direct approach and just ask. But you could try a little subterfuge," I said and got out of the van.

We waited after I knocked on the door since there was no doorbell. After a few moments, I knocked again. I heard movement inside and finally the door opened a crack, the chain still on. She asked what we wanted and I said we just needed some information about Troy Berlington. She hesitated then closed the door, I could hear the chain being removed and the door opened back up.

Before us stood a middle-aged blonde, heavy-set woman in a ratty robe, looking like she had just tumbled out of bed. She looked like death warmed over; sunken eyes darken by lack of sleep or something worse. Her hair was a mess reminding me of the Bride of Frankenstein and she was shaking slightly.

"Mrs. Petrocelli, I'm Jim Richards and this is Will Trapper, we're investigating the death of Troy Berlington, who I understand you knew."

"Knew? Oh hell yeah, I knew him. I knew him in the biblical sense too. The bastard used me and tossed me aside. I caught hell for knewing him from my husband. We finally got over it since Troy's death."

"Do you knew... sorry, know anything about his death?"

"You two want to come in and talk, fine. I can use friendly company." She turned and walked away from

113

the door. Trapper and I cautiously followed her in. She yelled from another room, "Either of you want coffee?"

We both declined and she came back in with a cup and said to sit. We went to a couple chairs in the living room and sat. I watched the woman as she paced the room looking like she was on the verge of having a nervous breakdown. She was shaking and sweating, even though the room was cool from the AC. She put the coffee cup down and finally sat. She was still acting as if she was waiting for something to happen.

"Are you alright Mrs. Petrocelli?" I asked.

"Hell no, I'm having a withdrawal from cocaine, you aren't cops are you? I don't have any drugs here."

"Uh, no we aren't police. You're an addict?"

"Was, that's why I'm having a withdrawal, genius. That bastard Berlington got me hooked on the crap, thankfully I've only been on it a couple months now so I may be able to beat it out of my system. My husband has been helping me through this. Bastard Berlington, I hope he rots in hell," she said.

She made a good point about hell, with Berlington going up in flames. "Mrs. Petrocelli, where were you the night Troy was murdered?"

"I was in the hospital, having just had a small seizure from a near overdose. I'm supposed to be on bed rest but people keep coming to the damn door."

"What people?"

"Those damn drug dealing friends of Troy's. He told them I had his stash, rat bastard."

"Have you called the police?"

"Are you serious? They would start asking too many questions about his dealings. I never helped him but I was around when he pulled that shit. Now his buddies and other junkies think I took over his business. My husband has gone out to get a gun to protect us."

"Was your husband with you the night you had your seizure?"

"Yes he was. He took me in and stayed with me the whole time."

I looked to Will and he just shrugged. "Troy was a dealer then?"

"He sure was and I'm sure he was torched by his competitors, he would tell me they were out to take over his territory."

Mrs. Petrocelli, did you know Charles Lawton?"

"Lawton? No, never heard of him."

"Okay, sorry to bother you. We'll let ourselves out." I stood followed by Trapper and we left the apartment.

"So, what do you think?" I asked once we were in the van.

"That woman is screwed up. I think she had more than a passing attraction to cocaine. I've seen too many cases of drug addiction in my long career of police work. She is deep into it."

"If she were deeper into drugs than she is admitting about Berlington, then what she said about him is suspect."

"I'd say so, but I think she was serious about not knowing Lawton. So there is still no connection I can see between Berlington and Lawton's murders."

"So what about the drug connection. Could Troy have been murdered by a rival drug dealer?"

"I'd say that's the first good bet. But again, where does Lawton fit in?"

"We need to bug Lynn about this. I see a trip to Metro in our immediate future," I said.

"Good, because I need to get to a computer," Trapper said with a grin.

We drove over to Metro and parked, going in the back way to Lynn's office. Trapper had to spend a little time talking to old friends, ones he knew when he was a cop here in Vegas years back.

We made our way to Lynn's office but she wasn't there. Warren was at his desk and said she called and she was on her way in. Trapper went right to her desk and opened up her computer.

"Should you be doing that?" I asked.

"When I worked here I had access to the computers so I know what I'm doing."

"Famous last words, just don't get caught."

I looked out to the squad room; it was empty except for Warren and a few interns doing paperwork. Trapper took out his camera, pulled the SD card and inserted it into the case of Lynn's computer. I knew what he was doing, getting into trouble.

He did a few things on the keyboard then finished up, pulling the card and putting the computer back to sleep. He stood, came around the desk and sat next to me. We waited for Lynn and Deacon to arrive.

They shuffled in about twenty minutes later and saw us. "Oh look Deacon, it's the Hardy Boys detective agency. Now what can we do for you?"

"Funny, and we're doing your work for you, that's gratitude," I said.

"When you start doing my work, I'll retire. What do you have?" She went to her chair behind the desk and sat, reached over and started her computer.

I told her briefly about our talk with Petrocelli and then asked, "Do you know or can find out if Lawton was into drugs?"

"I'll check on it," she said just as there was a loud laugh from the squad room. I looked out the office window and saw Warren laughing while looking at his computer. He saw Lynn watching and pointed to his computer and then to hers. She looked to her monitor and started laughing, then stopped.

"Will, you did this didn't you?" she said.

"Did what?"

"The pictures of Weber as Elvis you showed me, they're on the computer background instead of the Metro police logo. Weber is going to shit if he sees this." she paused and then said, "He doesn't know you saw him?"

"Nope, I took them from a distance."

She sat staring at the screen, "I'll pretend I hadn't seen this yet."

*

Chapter 16

Lynn ran a check on Charles Lawton and came up with nothing in the way of a criminal past. She called forensics and asked about the shell casing we found, she listened and hung up.

"They did manage to pull a partial print off the shell, but there's no match in the system. They're still trying to run it down. Did you talk to Morgan about Lawton?"

"He told me a little about him when I asked about the mystery woman. There was nothing special about Lawton, he performed around town and had a promising career for his impersonation of the king. He's from LA but has a place here that he maintains when he's in town. Can you get anything from LAPD on him?"

"I'll call a friend out there and see what Lawton may have on that end. So do you have some more info from the lover?"

"Yeah, as I explained briefly, Doris Petrocelli says that Berlington was a drug dealer and got her into cocaine, but Will thinks she's into it deeper."

"I've seen way too many women like her strung out on drugs, she was a heavy user on a crash," Trapper said.

"I'll check Berlington for priors on drug charges; that may be worth looking into. Possibly a rival dealer didn't like this guy, even if he was a good Elvis."

"That's the other thing, if he was so successful as an Elvis, why all the risk of running drugs?" I asked.

"Who knows, maybe he came from a broken past and found Elvis late in life," Deacon said.

"Like finding God in prison?" Trapper said.

Blue Suede Murders

"Something like that," I said, "but he didn't stop the drug usage according to Petrocelli. She also had every reason to kill him but she said she was in the hospital when he was torched, along with her husband." I thought about that, it's what she told us happened, but could she be lying? I'd have to check on it.

Lynn was typing on her keyboard and chuckling as she would see Weber on the screen. She sat reading from a file and looked to us. "It seems that Berlington was a bad boy. He was busted about two years ago for drug possession and sales. He assaulted a police officer while being arrested and was sentenced to two years. He got out in one year for good behavior and after... get this, finding Jesus. And Elvis." She printed out his sheet and handed it to me.

I was studying his mug shot along with his arrest record and then handed it to Trapper. He did his speed reading magic and handed it back to Lynn.

"So he started his Elvis career while in prison, talk about Jailhouse rock," I said, Lynn gave me a dirty look. "What?" I said. "He went from jail bird to strip performer in less than a year, he must have been good."

"According to Weber he was the King." She paused to carefully study Weber's picture on the computer. "Weber looks like a glittery beach ball in that getup. I'm surprised that no one knew about this."

"You don't think he's gone undercover to track the killer do you?" I asked.

"If he has, he never told any of us. I have a feeling he will have a heart attack when he sees this. Luckily he's off today, and we now know why."

I stood and said, "Well whatever he's up to, find out what you can about Lawton in LA and let me know, please." I looked to Trapper, "Shall we go rescue our merry band of Elvis lovers and go eat?"

"It's a plan," he said and followed me out of the room.

Lynn yelled to us, "Get me something I can give to Weber as he's torturing us."

I waved and kept going. We drove back toward the MGM, after I called Penny. They said they were on the strip by the Mirage Hotel and would meet us back at the MGM. I told her I had some inquiries to do and would be in the convention center.

We found Morgan and asked if he could talk, he said he was just relaxing. We went to sit in the auditorium, now empty.

"Morgan, did you know that Berlington was pushing drugs?" I asked.

He was quiet and then said, "I heard rumors, but I never confronted him about it. I didn't want trouble from him but I didn't like the drug connection to Elvis. You know the King was into drugs also. Berlington was subtle about it so I let it go."

"Did any of those rumors have anything to say about competitor drug dealers wanting him out of the business?"

"Do you think that's why he was killed?"

"Not sure, mostly because of Lawton's murder. Why were the two of them killed and a bunch of other Elvises threatened? If it were into the drugs, what is the connection to the other threats?"

"To cover the real reason for Berlington's murder? I don't know much about Lawton, other than he came from LA and worked here on and off."

"I wonder if Lawton may have been bringing drugs in from LA and Berlington was his connection here. It's something to think about."

"And a rival dealer didn't like either of them and threatened others to cover the killings?" Morgan said after thinking it over.

"I have another question, how did the killer get the names and phone numbers of all the Elvises he called to threaten?"

"That's easily explained, there is a directory of all the Elvises in our group. It covers all the details so members can contact others for bookings. If the killer had access to the directory, he would have all the numbers."

"Is this directory available to all members?"

"It is, there's nothing really private about it. We all agree to share our info for better communications within the group."

That was good enough for me. I was hoping for a better answer to help narrow down the people who could have access to the phone numbers.

"We talked to Doris Petrocelli and that is one messed up woman. Did you know much about her?"

"Just that her husband is a Dean Martin impersonator. He's out of town a lot because he's part of a touring Rat Pack show. Gave his wife a lot of time to screw around and Troy took advantage of it. Rumor has it she was a heavy drug user. Max Petrocelli had to put his wife in the hospital a few times when he was in town, to get her dried out. He didn't like Berlington even before he found out the wife was enjoying his company. Professional jealousy I guess."

"And when he found out, do you think he was capable of killing Burlington?"

"Sure, but why Lawton's murder?"

"That's the sore point right now and we need to find the common thread between them."

I heard a door open and looked over to see our group come in. Penny in the lead. She could always find me where ever I was.

"Hey Babe, how was your walk on the strip?" I asked.

"Hot. There wasn't much going on and we didn't have the time to go into a casino to visit, so we just walked watching the people. They have a new Elvis at Harrahs' now, replacing your flame broiled one."

"Really, that was fast." I looked to Morgan, he said, "They called and I recommend a new one, the show must go on."

"Well, if you hear any new rumors, let me know." I stood and asked everyone if they were hungry. They all said they were.

We went to the restaurant row and were seated in the same restaurant where Penny and I had our first dinner here when we came here for the convention of broadcast television. That was when Penny picked up her national show.

We were all comfortable and I asked, "Lacey, was it all worth it to go today?"

"Well I was hoping there would be a little more action, but it was all right," she said with a grin.

"Where's Mac today, it's Saturday?"

"He's with Jessie, they're bonding over at Circus, Circus and then going to a new water park. He tries to give her as much time as he can. Buck keeps him busy with supervising the guards. I hardly see him myself."

Jessie was a teenager whose father was killed by the Vegas vigilante a while back and Penny and I took her in until Lacey and Mac where married and then they became her foster parents.

"Well I can talk to Buck and see if he can ease up on Mac."

"No that's all right, when Mac finally finds time for me, it's really good." She started to turn red again, that meant she was referring to sex. I laughed and she got redder.

"Take a breath Lacey, we're all friends here." I looked to Val and Blake, "Are you two getting anxious to get married?"

"Yes, we are ready for the commitment. It's the bond that holds us together," Val said.

Trapper laughed and said, "I was never one to want to be committed, too restrictive."

Penny whacked Trapper on the arm, he flinched, "Why'd you do that?"

"I don't want you scaring these two. So just hold your opinions."

"Yes, Ma'am," he said.

"Now, have you got the trail of the killer?" Penny asked changing the subject.

"Well, my dear I'm very suspicious of you. Where were you yesterday around noon when Lawton was murdered?"

"I was busy rethinking my marriage to you."

*

Chapter 17

We drove Lacey back to the office where she left her car. She said she was going to track down Mac and Jessie to join them. I took the rest of the crew back to our home; we all piled out of the van and went straight through the house to the pool. Penny and Val had gone off to change into swimsuits so Trapper, Blake and I sat waiting for them. Willy was already in the pool as I kept an eye on him. The girls came out and went in swimming back and forth, as we admired them.

"So where are we going now?" Trapper asked me.

"Well, it would be nice to know about Lawton more. Plus, I want to check on Doris Petrocelli's claim to have been in the hospital during Berlington's murder. I should have asked her which hospital."

"Yeah, some detective you are," Trapper said with a smirk. "I have a friend in LV Medical who may help on that. I'll call her and see if she can find out anything."

"Thanks, may as well wait till Monday to see. The Elvis convention ends then, with the big judging of the best Elvis of show later in the evening. Should be interesting to see who wins, we may need to look into his background," I said.

My cell phone rang and I saw it was Lynn. "Hey, what's shaking?"

"The earth, when Weber gets back. Now I have some interesting news about Lawton." She paused, and then said, "There is no Lawton in LA, he technically doesn't exist."

"Okay so who is the man who was shot?"

"His name is Gustove Schmit, not Charles Lawton. He took a stage name for his work as Elvis and that's why we couldn't find any background on him."

"How did you find this out?" I asked.

"My friend in LAPD is an Elvis follower and had investigated Lawton back when there was a charge of assault when he attacked a man in the audience who was heckling. They got his real name from his driver's license and he was booked under that name. My friend said he has a background in petty larceny and fraud. No drug charges were found, but he's got a record."

"Interesting, I wonder if Morgan knows about this, or is just hiding the facts. So many Elvises with shady pasts, makes you wonder. Do you know what the fraud charges involved?"

Blue Suede Murders

"Seems he sold some paintings to someone saying they were real and they weren't. The buyer pressed charges and Lawton/ Schmit, spent a short time in jail."

"Where he discovered Jesus and Elvis?"

"No, he was doing Elvis before that; he's been in it for about two years.

"Can you do me a favor? Can you look up Max Petrocelli and see what you have on him?"

"The Dean Martin impersonator? What does he have to do with this?"

"He's married to the blonde bimbo who was messing with Berlington. I just want to cover all bases so I can get a connection to them all."

"I'll give him a run and see what he's got and call you."

I thanked her and hung up. "Well, the plot thickens, seems Charles Lawton wasn't who he said he was," I said to Trapper. "His real name was Gustove Schmit, and he has a rap sheet but not for drugs"

"I can see why he would change his name, not the best for an Elvis impersonator. Ladies and Gentlemen, Gustove Schmit as Elvis. Nope, doesn't work for me."

"I asked Lynn to check on Doris Petrocelli's husband to see if he has a record. Just to tie up a few loose ends."

I heard the side gate open and Angelo came in the yard. "Hey big guy, what's happening?"

"Not much Mr. R., I was just resting when I heard yous guys out here. Catch da killer yet?"

"Sorry, no. We're still at it."

Blake stood and asked Angelo if he could talk to him. They went off the side of the yard where I couldn't hear them. I was wondering what plot Blake was cooking up. I could see Angelo nodding and then he broke out in a big smile and gave Blake a bear hug. They came back.

"What's up with you two?" I asked.

Blake smiled and said, "Ah just asked Angelo to be ma best man. Ah may need his strong muscles ta hold me up when I marry Val."

"Well congratulations Angelo, that will be nice."

I asked him to join us and he sat. "Angelo, do you have any connections in LA?"

"I know a few people, whatcha need?"

"Nothing right now, but maybe later. Just some info and you're good at that."

Blue Suede Murders

"Thanks Mr. R., I like helping yous guys."

Penny came swimming over and said hello to Angelo, he beamed and said hello back. "I talked to Mom this morning," he said.

"How is Francis?" Penny asked.

"She's good and says she may come out to visit next month, she's getting bored back in New York."

"Well, tell her that I'll take her around to see the town better this time than last."

"I will."

I stood and said I was going in the house for refreshments since it was getting late, time for a beer. Trapper jumped up and came with me leaving Blake and Angelo to chat. The two of them with their different ways of speaking, Blake's southern dialect and Angelo's mob vernacular would be interesting to hear, but I heard a can of beer calling my name first.

Trapper and I were in the kitchen and he said, "I'm wondering if Max may have killed Berlington for screwing his wife, then did the hit on Lawton to cover his motive."

"I was thinking that also, Max was in the circle of impersonators and may have even known of Lawton's shady past. He figures he'd bump them both off and cover his ass."

"What say we track him down and see what he has to say?"

"Okay, tomorrow morning we'll go visit the strung out Mrs. Petrocelli and talk to hubby."

"Deal, I'll be here early."

"Just not before nine, please. I hear that driveway alarm go off any earlier, I may meet you at the door with my Glock."

"Hey, I gave you that gun back when you graduated from PI school. Remember?"

"Yes, I do, thanks. It has been a life saver on a couple occasions."

We all finished the evening with refreshments then Trapper said he had to go. I asked if he could drop Val and Blake at the MGM Grand and he said he would. Angelo said he was tired and went to the guesthouse. They were all gone and Penny was straightening out the back yard. I was in the kitchen looking out the window at her still in her bikini. I pulled off my clothes and snuck up behind her grabbing on and we both tumbled into the pool. She screamed in surprise and we came up laughing. I undid her bikini strings and we... well, you know what.

Early next morning right at nine, the driveway alarm went off, I had to hand it to Trapper, he was punctual. I met him at the door and he came in.

Blue Suede Murders

"Good morning Will," Penny said as she breezed by us into the kitchen where Angelo was making breakfast. I told Trapper to sit at the snack bar as Angelo asked him if he would he like some pancakes.

"I haven't had homemade pancakes since my mother used to make them; that would be real nice."

"Angelo is going to open a restaurant; I think he should call it Food Like Mom Used to Make. How's that sound?"

Angelo laughed loudly and said that sounded good to him. I sat next to Trapper and said, "We can go check on Max and then see if Lynn has anything more on Lawton."

We had our breakfast then Penny said she was going to pick up Val and Blake and they were going to explore the malls. I felt for Blake. Penny left and Angelo went off to go to church. I hadn't been to church since I was a kid and my parents dragged me in. They stopped going after a while from being disappointed by our minister, he was such a hypocrite.

"So shall we go track down Dean Martin?" Trapper asked.

"I'm ready."

We drove out again to Doris Petrocelli's residence and parked. I sat looking at the building and hoped her husband was in.

"Last time we were here, Doris said her husband was getting a gun, we should proceed with caution," I said.

"I'm way ahead of you. I took the safety off my gun. Shall we?"

We exited the car and went to the door, knocking again and waiting. After a few minutes, the door opened a crack, chain on, and it was Doris. "What do you two want now?" she said.

"Just need to talk to your husband, if he's home?"

She hesitated then opened the door after removing the chain. "You can come in but Max isn't here."

"Do you know where we can find him?"

"He's back out on the road with his show. Out in Alabama now I think."

"You're looking much better now, how are you feeling?" Trapper asked.

"I'm okay, just still getting through it."

"By the way, which hospital did you and your husband go to when Berlington was murdered?" I asked.

She hesitated, "Why?"

"We just need to firm up all persons involved. You do know you had motive to murder Troy and your husband had motive also. We need to clear you of the crime with an alibi."

She hesitated again, "LV Medical, but Max didn't want the publicity so he registered under an assumed name and paid by cash."

"What name was that?" I asked.

"I don't know, Max did it, you have to ask him."

I looked to Trapper, I was sure he was thinking the same thing. The woman was covering something.

*

Chapter 18

Most drug addicts weren't that good at covering their lies, Doris wasn't very good at it either.

"Doris, you know that we can track down your alibi for the murder, so do you want to stick with the hospital story?"

She looked nervous now and stood, "I don't like your insinuations; I think you should leave now." She went to the door, opened it and stood waiting. I shrugged to Trapper and we got up.

Bob Moats

I stopped at the door behind Trapper, "It will come out, Doris. If you have something to say, do it now or it will be too late."

She stood defiantly and said nothing. We left and she slammed the door. I looked to Trapper and said, "This is something to look more into. Can we find the agency that books Max's trips?"

"I know who to ask. Come on." He went back to the van and he directed me to a small office building by the Stratosphere. "It's Sunday, think anyone would be here?" I asked.

"Hell, these people don't care what day it is, there's work all across the country and these people handle the touring companies. They work seven days a week."

We went into the small but well arranged lobby and Trapper went to the receptionist.

"Hi, is Jerry Klein in?"

"Who shall I say is calling?"

"Will Trapper."

She picked up the phone and called, listened and then a man came out from a side door.

"Wow, Will Trapper, I haven't seen you in years. How the hell are you?"

Blue Suede Murders

"Good, you haven't broken any laws lately have you?"

He gave us a grin and said, "I've been a model citizen since you last arrested me. I quit drinking and getting mean with people. It wasn't worth the hassle. What can I do for you?" he asked as he led us to an office. He motioned for us to sit and he went behind an oversized desk making him look small.

"Jerry, do you or someone here book the Rat Pack touring show with Max Petrocelli?"

"We sure do, our best attraction, all over the country. Booked months in advance. What do you need to know about them?"

"Are they out on tour now and is Max with them?"

"Funny you ask that, they are out on tour, but Max is AWOL. He can't be reached and his wife says he's on some personal job in California. I don't question it, we have plenty of replacements for him. Everyone thinks he can be Deano. Max wasn't even the best but he works for the wages we give him. Money is tight nowadays, so there has been a cut back in salaries. I just figured Max found a better deal."

Trapper looked to me and winked. "So the final word is that Max is missing."

"I guess you could say that, I haven't heard from him."

They talked briefly about what they had done since they last saw each other, then Trapper excused us to go back to investigating. We left the building and back into the van, just sitting.

"So going over this, Berlington is murdered, blonde girlfriend's husband didn't like what he was doing to his wife, murders Troy and then Lawton to put the blame on some Elvis hater and then skips the state for a while. Sound right to you?" Trapper asked.

"I'd say Max is our main suspect now, shall we share this with Lynn?"

"I'd say so, let's go see if Weber has discovered his pictures yet."

I drove over to Metro and parked. We entered and went straight to Lynn's office. She was staring at the computer and typing, then she saw us and sighed. "Weber hasn't been in yet, just waiting. Will, can you take this off the computer before he hangs someone?" Just as she said that, there came a roar from the front of the building in the direction of Weber's office. Lynn frowned, "Too late, I think he knows."

We could hear him storming and cursing in the hallway. "I want the perpetrator of this prank, someone will die!" He came back to where we were and saw Trapper.

"Ah ha, you did this! I don't know how but you are behind it, I just know."

"Morning Captain, what are you talking about?" Trapper said quietly.

"You know damn well, my private life is not for exhibition here at the station! Now take that off immediately or I'll have you arrested for tampering with police property!" He stormed off.

"Elvis has left the room," I said

We all were quietly laughing as Lynn got up and pointed Trapper to her computer. He went to sit and about five minutes later, he had restored the computer.

"Okay now that we are finished torturing Weber, what do you want?" Lynn asked.

"We have some info and a theory," I started. We explained to her what we found and she was happy with the results.

"I'll go fill Weber in and maybe that will placate him." She left the room and we sat.

"So what are you planning on doing with the pictures of Weber now? I'm sure you aren't done yet," I said.

"I'm just beginning." He smiled.

Lynn came back and said, "Weber is happy and I even gave you two the credit; so he may not press charges," she said with a laugh.

"Now you should go bring in Doris Petrocelli for questioning," Trapper said.

"Weber is sending a car to pick her up. Thanks for the information. I hope this settles the case. Weber is also putting out a warrant for Max on suspicion of murder."

"Great, let us know what you come up with; I think we need to go to the convention center to do a final bit of business."

"Not fully convinced that this is the solution?" Lynn asked.

"I'm happy with what we have, but I owe it to Morgan to fill him in. He did hire me to investigate and I'll remind him of that fact. I can use the pay," I said with a grin.

"What do I get out of this?" Trapper asked.

"My undying gratitude," I said.

"Not hardly worth it," he said and stood. We went back out to the van and drove over the MGM Grand.

We found Morgan in the auditorium getting things ready for the big show. He saw us and came over.

"So have you found the killer yet?" he asked.

"We have a suspect and a warrant out for him."

"Anyone I know?"

Blue Suede Murders

"Max Petrocelli."

"I had a feeling you were going to say that. He was high on my list of people to suspect. Do you know where he is?"

"Nope, we hope he's not too far away, and his wife is being taken in for questioning."

"Well thanks for filling me in. You think the killings will stop now?"

"Has anyone else been threatened lately?"

"Nope it's been quiet, no phone calls and no threats. I hope this is it now, it looks bad for our group."

"Well we may have solved the case, I'll send you the bill when we have Max in custody," I said with a grin.

"I'll turn it into our accounting, thanks. Now I have to get the big show set up, are you coming?"

"Wouldn't miss it, thanks and see you later." He went off and we went to the lobby of the hotel and were watching all the tourist moving about, especially the women. My cell phone rang and it was Lynn.

"Did you find Doris?" I asked.

"Yep, she was still at her home, but she was dead. You did leave her alive right?"

I was shocked and looked to Trapper, said to him,

"Doris is dead." Then I asked Lynn, "How?"

"Had her throat cut, did you see anyone else in her place?"

"No, just her. But anyone could have been there. I'm thinking Max may not be that far away. But why would he kill his wife?"

"You're the big detective, you tell me." She laughed.

"Maybe he was afraid she would talk, but at this time it's really a moot point. We already have radar on him, time will tell."

"Can you come back in to make your statement official on what she said?"

"Sure we'll be back shortly." I hung up and said to Trapper, "I don't like talking to people who turn up dead. It's a creepy feeling."

"I know having been in homicide for years and seeing all the bodies, it gets to you after a while."

"Well Lynn wants us back to give our statements, shall we go?"

We went back to Metro and in to find Lynn talking to Joe Lang., ME. We came up and Joe greeted us.

"Hey Will, how you been?"

"Good, what's up in the morgue?"

"No one I hope. It gets a little scary down there at times. I have a mystery."

Lynn took us into her office and we sat. Joe cleared his throat and spoke.

"Ok, I was performing the autopsy on the body of Berlington and found something strange. There was a metal rod and pin in his right leg and some old wounds on his torso. Some of the signs, even though the body was burned to a virtual crisp, where that this body was of an older man, not one of Berlington's age. I managed to get hold of some dental records of Berlington and they don't match, the few teeth left weren't burnt that badly even though the fire was hot enough to destroy most of the body."

Lynn said, "So the body in Berlington's caddie wasn't him?"

"That's it in a nut shell. I'm not ruling it was him. This guy was dressed in the costume but not him. I haven't any idea who the body is but the rod and pin in the leg may help. I'll run a check on hospital records for that type of operation if it was done around here and serial numbers off the rod."

"Thanks Joe, this is getting weird now. Doris is dead and we have an unknown in the morgue who is supposed to be an Elvis. If it wasn't, who was it?"

"I hope to find out, this also means that Berlington is not dead like we thought," Joe said.

"This a new twist, where is Berlington?" I said.

*

Chapter 19

"Now I'm wondering if Berlington may be behind this," I said.

"It's a new thought. I'm not going to Weber with this until we identify the body in the morgue," Lynn said, "he's still in a foul mood about the pictures." She gave Trapper a look and he smiled at her.

"Joe can you check to see if the body could be Max Petrocelli?" I asked.

"The Dean Martin impersonator? Why him?"

"It's a long story but he's missing and he's our number one suspect for the killing of... well whoever is in the morgue," Lynn said. "Just see if Petrocelli had any operations on his leg."

"Sure I'll check and I'll let you know." He stood and went out.

Lynn just sat back and sighed deeply. "This is not a good day. Deacon is in a mood and we are not speaking, my fault, I have been cranky lately and he has taken most the brunt of it from me. I need to make it up to him."

"He has been a little tense that I've noticed. Maybe just some time off for the both of you to get away and find each other again."

She was quiet and said, "Yeah, that sounds good, I'll have a talk with him when he calms down."

Trapper laughed and said, "Deacon would get in these moods back in Michigan when he worked in my precinct. I'd send him out to take a couple days off and go fishing. He used to enjoy that. Maybe you should suggest a fishing trip?"

"Ugg, fish. Well, if it makes him happy, I'll try it. But I need to finish this case first before we can do anything. Weber would never approve time off for either of us until we catch the Elvis killer."

"Go camping and fishing over at Lake Mead, that would be nice." I offered.

"Thanks, I'll keep that in mind."

"Let us know, now I think we need to go throw this new revelation at Morgan and see what he says about it." We finished and Trapper and I left the building.

I was getting tired of driving to the MGM Grand but we had to talk to Morgan again. I parked in the structure and sat for a minute. Trapper asked what I was doing.

"I'm organizing my thoughts, and I need to check on Penny to make sure she hasn't spent all our money at the mall." I pulled my cell phone and called, she came on quickly.

"Hey Sweetie, did you catch the killer yet?"

"No, and we are getting deeper into a mystery. Seems the body in the Cadillac we thought was Berlington wasn't him, and the girlfriend turned up dead."

"I think it's Berlington, he did it all. Burned someone to look like him and then disappeared after killing the girlfriend so she wouldn't talk. How did I do?"

I was amazed how she could cut through the crap to the most likely lead. "You did good Babe. How's the shopping?"

"Good, Blake is going crazy with us, but we are being nice to him and letting him buy some nice Vegas clothing."

I cringed at that thought and said that was nice. "I am back at the MGM, so we'll be here a while, I'll talk to you later." She said goodbye and we disconnected.

"Okay lets go find Morgan," I said to Trapper.

We found him in the auditorium and called him over. He excused himself from the men he was talking to and walked down the stage stairs and over to us.

"You're back, got some new information? This is getting exciting being in on the investigation."

"Yep, got some new information, Berlington isn't dead," I said when he was near.

"What? I thought he was burnt up in his caddie? How could he be alive?"

"That's what we need to find out now. Someone was in his car when he was doused with liquid and set ablaze, but we don't know who it was yet. The coroner is doing some investigating and hopefully will have some info.

"Wow, this is interesting. Berlington can't perform now, it would be too odd and I'm sure the police would want to talk to him. So where would he go?"

"I was hoping you may have an idea on that? Where would he go? You said you knew him."

"I didn't know him that well. I don't even know who his friends are. He wasn't very open about his life. I can ask around the group, it may help."

"I think that is a good idea, we need to get a bunch of them together and talk. Can you find a few to start?"

"Sure I'll have them in the OZ room again, let me arrange it." I agreed and he went off.

I turned to Trapper, "Berlington is still nearby, I can feel it. He has an agenda and this isn't over. I'm a little concerned for this big show tonight," I said.

"I understand what you're saying. Maybe we need the police protection again?"

"I don't think it will do a lot of good, just make it harder on him to do what he is trying to accomplish. Let go to OZ and see what we can find."

"I'm sure it won't be Dorothy and her damn dog Toto," Trapper laughed.

We went to the room and found about ten Elvi, plural. They were all joking and talking as we came in and then they went quiet. I said to go on with what they were doing. Morgan came in with two more men and said to me, "All these men knew Berlington, so I hope they will cooperate with you."

I went to the front of the group and said, "Sorry to take your time from the convention but we need some help. As you all know Troy Berlington was murdered the other day in a car on the strip, along with Charles Lawton here at the convention. Now the kicker is, Troy Berlington was not murdered." I waited to see the reaction, just a lot of murmur and surprised looks. "The body in the caddie was not him, we are trying to identify the body but we know it was not Berlington. Now you can help, we need to know who Troy may have been friends with, names and locations would be a big help. Anyone want to start?"

It reminded me of a funeral parlor, everyone sitting looking stone faced. Finally, one young Elvis stood and said, "I knew him, he was a mentor to me. I am happy he's still alive, but I couldn't tell you where he would be. Not that I won't, I just don't know. I also

147

can't say why he would be hiding out, if that's what he's doing. Honestly, he had drug problems, and maybe he is hiding out from people he doesn't want to know he's alive. It makes sense to me." He sat back down.

"Fine, but how does he go on now, he can't perform in Vegas anymore. He'd have to leave the state to work elsewhere. Could that be an option?" I asked.

The young Elvis was quiet then another man spoke, "Berlington was evil, I admired him for his performances but off stage he was a bastard and didn't care who he got on drugs. I wasn't going to be the one to rat him out back then, but this is ridiculous. If he's still alive he is probably still in the drug pipeline. I know a few of us can give you the information you need to track him down." He stood turned to the other men and continued, "How many times did he give drugs to young people who worshiped him. If you stay silent you are just as bad as he was. I'm not hiding him anymore." He turned to me and said, "I'll help."

There were two more men who voiced their desire to help. I asked everyone who couldn't help to leave. All but four left. I had the four come up and sit in front and called Lynn.

She was there in a hurry, "I just left Weber and he is really messed up. His hero is alive but maybe the killer. This is not good. What do you have?"

"These men all want to help in giving their information on Berlington's activities. I'll turn it over to you."

She stood in front of the men and asked what they had. Turning to the first man on the right, "What do you know?"

"Berlington could have been a legend but he was deep into drugs. Selling, pushing, distributing, he did it all. He wanted money, lots of it. I looked away when he would push his shit on people. I'm ashamed for it, but I don't know why this is happening. Or where he may be." He went silent and Lynn thanked him.

She went to the next man, "What do you have?"

He squirmed a bit then said, "I agree with Harry about the drugs and stuff. Troy had a girlfriend out in Henderson. He was working out of her house."

"Do you know where she lives?"

"No, I was never there, but her name was Lucy something, she had an arrest record from what I understand. That may help."

"Anyone else know this Lucy something from Henderson?" she asked of the group.

Silence again, then one man on the other end spoke, "Lucy Parson, lives on Chatsworth, don't know the address."

"I won't ask how you know her, just thank you for the info."

*

Chapter 20

Lynn had called Weber giving him the new information on the possible location of Berlington and asked for a search warrant. He agreed to start the ball on his end and make a call for it.

Deacon was on his phone calling for backup and gave them the address they got from Williams in the precinct. He told them to gather at the location, but to hold back until Lynn and he showed up in case they got there first.

Trapper and I went out to my van and sat waiting for them to start so we could follow them down to Henderson to the gated community where Lucy Parsons lived. I was hoping Berlington would be there and bring this to an end.

Trapper said, "Do you think he'll be there?"

"I don't know but he has to be somewhere, it's a good start. Maybe if this Lucy is there she will tell us more. I'm starting to see the pattern for the crime, but we still need to hook Lawton in."

"He had a record, probably got into Troy's clutches and may have been close to ratting him out. Time will tell." We saw everyone file out of the station and to their cars, driving out and down to Henderson.

We pulled up to the guard shack and Lynn flashed her badge and the sentry opened the gate. She stopped and asked if any other cops had arrived yet, he said no. She warned him that plenty of cars would be coming shortly so be ready on the gate. He acknowledged her and we went in. I was behind Lynn and we parked around the corner of the street were Parsons lived. We waited for both the warrant and the backup.

Lynn and Deacon came back to my van and got in. Lynn sat in the passenger captain's chair, looked around at the interior and said, "Damn this thing is comfy."

"I like it. What are you charging Berlington with if we find him here?" I asked.

"Suspicion of murder and conspiracy to commit fraud. He made out another person to look like him, so he had to be hiding something." Lynn's cell phone rang, she answered, and she listened, then hung up.

"Surprise, Joe Lang tracked down a hospital record for Max Petrocelli, he had leg surgery to reconstruct broken leg bones from a car accident. Max is our crispy critter."

"So maybe Troy and the blonde bimbo plotted to do away with Max and then Troy did away with her," I said. "But why pretend to have Max as Troy in the fire?"

"I'd say Troy wants to go underground, change his life and start new. That's all I can figure," Lynn said.

Trapper was watching out the window and said that the backup had arrived. We got out of the van and she gathered the men to explain what was going down. One man had the paperwork for the warrant and Lynn said they were good to go. They all got back in their cars and flew around the corner to the house pulling up on the driveway and lawn.

The officers ran to the front of the house as Lynn and Deacon went to the front door. She had two men go around the back and then banged on the door. They all waited and after a couple more poundings, the door opened and there stood a woman barely five foot nothing and looking like she just got out of the shower.

"Are you Lucy Parson?" Lynn asked.

"I am," she said quietly looking shocked at all the police.

"Please step aside, we have a search warrant for the premises." Lynn let the officers go by and then took the woman aside. "Do you know Troy Berlington and is he here?"

She looked like she was wrestling with her answer.

"Not hard to say, yes you know him and he's here."

"No he's not here; he was killed a couple days ago."

"That's how you want to answer? We know it wasn't him in the torched car. Now you want to tell us where he is?"

She was quiet again. I could hear the officers yelling clear throughout the place, and then one voice called for Lynn. She told a uniform to watch the woman and we went in the direction of the call.

We entered what looked like a family room but it was filled with paraphernalia for making meth. Lynn yelled to be cautious in the room; it was filled with dangerous gases. She left the room and got on her cell to call CSI and the bomb squad to dispose of the dangerous parts of the equipment.

"I love it when a plan comes together," she said with a big smile. "Now to grill Lucy in the sky with methamphetamines."

We went back to where Lucy was and Lynn took her to a smaller living room just off the vestibule. She had her sit and sat in front of her. "Lucy, you are in so much trouble. You don't want to go down for all this alone do you? So where's Berlington?"

She was looking really scared now, "You don't know the kind of people involved in this. If I talk, I'm dead. Yes, Troy is still alive, but I don't know where he is right now."

"Does he stay here?"

Blue Suede Murders

"He stays here and a couple other places, don't ask, I don't know where."

Lynn looked to Deacon and said, "Go to the gate and talk to the guard, they are supposed to know who comes and goes. They may know when he was last here and how often he comes. Then put someone near the gate in case he shows."

Deacon acknowledged her and went off. Lynn turned back to Lucy. "We will get him eventually, you can make it easier on all of us if you just cooperate."

"I can't, my life is worthless if I talk." She lifted her t-shirt and showed numerous burns across her stomach. "This is what he does when I screw up."

"He can't hurt you if you are in protective custody. We'll protect you."

"It's not just him; it's the scum he hangs with, those other Elvises."

That peaked our attention. "There are other Elvis impersonators involved?"

She paused then said, "Two others, I don't know their names but they come here and pick up drugs Troy has. They're creeps and talk rough, one of them beat up on Troy when he was short on their order. I was hiding in the closet when it happened. They left and I had to help Troy. I don't want to get involved."

"Well Lucy you are involved. Manufacturing of meth is a prison offense. Unless you can help us. Do you know how to get hold of Troy?"

"I have a number I can call in emergency, but if he finds out I gave it to you."

"Will you stop that! We'll protect you, We need to stop him and the others. Now what is the number?"

She stood and went to a desk in the room and picked up a small paper from the top drawer. She gave it to Lynn, there was a number scrawled across the center with no other info. Lynn said to a uniform to take Lucy into the precinct and watch her closely. Two officers escorted her out of the room and through the front door.

"I'll do a reverse look up and see where this goes, but it's probably a cell phone."

"Can I try something?" I asked. She hesitated then asked what.

"I'll call him on the house phone, he'll recognize the number and I'll make a threat that I have his girl and his meth lab, if he wants to save either, he better get here."

She thought a minute and nodded, "It may work, we need to get everyone out of here and hide nearby so we don't spook him." She stood and called to her men. She told them the plan and to go hide the cars around the subdivision away from the house until we see if we can get him here. They left and we got the house ready.

Blue Suede Murders

I went to the phone in the living room and Lynn gave me the number. I dialed and cleared my throat, trying to concentrate on how Angelo would make threats and tone my voice to that.

The phone rang and after about four rings someone answered. "Yeah," was all the voice said.

"Hey Troy boy, your girl was real cooperative when we convinced her to talk. She may be able to walk again, with therapy."

"Who the hell is this?"

"Never mind Troy, we got your meth lab too, we may just tie your woman in the middle of the room and blow the whole fucking place up. You got a smart answer now?"

"I'll kill you when I find you!" The voice yelled.

"Yeah, big fucking man. I'll be a nice guy and give you 30 minutes to get here so we can negotiate the safe return of your property. It does us no good to put you out of business, we need each other, but I can stop you in your tracks, 29 minutes and counting asshole." I hung up and looked to Lynn and Trapper.

"Not an Academy Award winning performances but I liked the voice you used. It may work."

Lynn called Deacon and told him the plan and to watch for him to arrive at the gate and warn the guards to act normal. Deacon said he'd just sit in the guard shack since Berlington didn't know him. Lynn said that would work and hung up.

"Now we wait."

*

Chapter 21

About twenty minutes later, Lynn's cell phone buzzed and she put it on speaker. It was Deacon saying loudly, "Three cars just blew through the gate arm, the guard is having fits. They're coming fast." Lynn hung up and turned to Warren and said, "Call Williams and tell him to have the cars ready to roll on my command and keep the line open."

She went to the men who she had stay back and said to go cover all the windows and then sent three uniforms to the back of the house, just in case.

I was carefully watching out the front window when I saw the cars come screaming up. "Berlington is a crazy fool after I threatened to blow the house up. Does he think he can storm the building and not get blown up?"

"Let's just focus on the immediate problem, they have automatic weapons," Trapper said as he watched six men get out of the cars. Lynn yelled to Warren to call the troops back. He told Williams to bring them in, with guns ready.

Lynn and Warren went by the front door as we

backed them up from down the hallway. We were ready for them to come bursting in just as the first volley of gunfire hit the door opening holes all over it.

We all ducked and waited as the door flew open but no one was there. Suddenly a flash bomb was thrown from around the door jam and we all spread out. The incendiary went off with its blinding flash and explosion knocking us off balance.

We brought ourselves around as two men entered the house spraying the room with their automatic weapons. Luckily, we were off in a side room and they were concentrating on the hallway to the kitchen.

Lynn and her men fired on the two intruders just inside the doorway and brought them down. I didn't see the other four men who were still out front. I started hearing gunfire from the back of the house, just as the front windows were being shot out.

I heard sirens as the five patrol cars were arriving and the gunfire out front was turned on them. I carefully looked out one of the front windows and could see three men firing at the uniforms as they were shooting from behind their cars. Two men went down and the other man ran off the to side of the building. I yelled to Lynn that one went around the left of the house and she went to the back.

All the cops out front had followed the man as one officer was checking the men on the ground. I was watching him and then looked past him to see someone sitting in the driver's seat of one of the bad guy's cars.

Bob Moats

I had seen a picture of Berlington from his rap sheet in Lynn's office, so I knew it was him. He was just sitting watching and then he started the car and backed out fast. I dialed Deacon hoping he was still at the guardhouse, he came on and I asked if he was still there. He said he was watching for any more cars arriving. I told him that Berlington was driving back out. He said he'd watch for him and I hung up, running to Lynn and told her.

She called to Warren and they ran to the front door and found her car. I went out and stood on the front lawn with Trapper following me as we could hear the gunshots from the back of the house, then it went quiet.

Williams came around the side and said they stopped them all and asked where Lynn was. I told him and he ran to his car to call on the radio for her location.

I turned to Trapper and said, "That was fun."

He just gave me a grin and said, "Hell of a nice way to spend an afternoon."

About an hour later, Lynn was back to the house; Berlington had managed to elude them.

"Well, it was a good try. We definitely know Berlington is alive now. Two of his men were only wounded so we can question them at least."

Deacon was escorting one of the survivors of the gunfight and sat him on a chair in the kitchen where we all stood. The man was in pain from a shoulder wound that looked to be been temporarily patched. Lynn went to him and said, "I hope you aren't making plans for your future slick, because I know where you are going to be spending it. Clark County Correctional jail. Ever been there, it's a hellhole, lots of gangbangers and punks like you and plenty of big angry guards who love it when the prisoners misbehave. Have you ever seen the restraint chair? I'll see that you are strapped into it with your head covered by the spit guard."

The man looked like a low life crud, as he sat silently. "Screw you," he said quietly.

"Well, it speaks." She turned to Warren and said to have a couple uniforms take him to the station to sweat it out in holding. Warren took care of that as Lynn, Deacon, Trapper and I went to the front of the house. CSI was back on the scene to finish going over the house. The meth lab had been dismantled for anything explosively dangerous to our health by the bomb squad. The house was now halfway quiet.

"So what now that we know Berlington is alive?" Deacon asked.

"He had to have torched Max in the caddie to establish his death. He was hiding out from someone, probably another drug dealer or a bigger cartel. He may have killed Doris Petrocelli because he murdered her husband and she may have wanted to expose him," Lynn said.

"You're guessing on that? Right?" I said.

160

"You got it Magnum. That's the way I see it, and I don't have much else to go on since the P.I. I hired to get me some info hasn't come across yet."

"Hey, I found Lucy Parsons didn't I?"

"Okay, I'll give you that. Now get me some reason for Berlington to be alive."

"Can I question the men we caught today?"

"You can share the interrogation. Shall we go?"

"Can I watch the carnage?" Trapper asked.

"Only if you don't say another word the rest of the day," Lynn replied.

"That's going to be difficult," I said as I followed Lynn and Deacon out the front door.

"Hey, I can be quiet. I'll just watch and still solve this case," Trapper said.

Trapper and I got into my van, which was parked around the corner and followed the parade back to Metro. On the way, I called Penny on my Bluetooth earpiece wirelessly connected to my phone.

"Hey Sweetie, what are you up to?" she asked when she answered.

"Oh I was just in the middle of a big gun fight with drug dealers and now we're going to beat them into telling us about the Elvis killer."

Blue Suede Murders

"That's nice, was it a fun gun fight?"

"Only the best, four dead bad guys and no good guys killed. But the leader got away. We're going to interrogate the two survivors to find out what is going on. How's your mall shopping?"

"We finished an hour ago and are back at the house, swimming of course. When are you coming home?"

"As I said, we're going to interrogate the bad guys to find Berlington so when we are finished, I'll be home."

"Okay, have a nice interrogation, don't hurt yourself beating them silly," she said and hung up.

I have to laugh at Penny's blasé attitude sometimes. It was something that endeared her to me.

Lynn told me they had to book and process the men before we could question them, so I swung through a Burger King and got some quick food to eat on the way.

We arrived back at Metro and went to interrogations. Lynn had the two survivors in separate rooms waiting for her questioning.

We waited outside in the squad room as Lynn stalled for time to make them sweat it out in the hot rooms. She had an uniform turn up the thermostat so it was nice and toasty. We could see the sweat from the man in the room closest to us.

"I have to get something for Weber, he's hot to nab Berlington now since it turned out he wasn't killed and may be the killer," Lynn said. She went to the first door and waved us to observation. We went in the small air-conditioned room and sat facing the tricky mirror. The hood was sitting back in his chair with his one arm out being handcuffed to the table restraints. Lynn entered followed by Deacon and they sat across from the man.

"Jerry Weiss, according to your rap sheet. You are a low level drug runner, is that a skill you learned in school?"

"Fuck you," he said.

Deacon slammed his fist onto the table, causing Weiss to jump. "Shut the hell up with your smart mouth. You have a big problem, use of deadly force with automatic weapons and possession of narcotics. We don't have to talk to you, you are roasted, but we may make a deal with you or your buddy in the other room for his information about Berlington."

"I know you are playing us off each other and it won't work," he said with a smirk.

Lynn looked to Deacon and said, "He's got us, we can't fool him. Let's go talk to Harry in the other room, maybe he'll make a deal and spill his guts to save his neck." Lynn stood and started to the door followed by Deacon.

The man sat quietly, then just before they got out the door he yelled, "What kind of deal?"

*

Chapter 22

"Okay Jerry, let's say you give us some useful info and we'll see if we can get your charges lowered, maybe even dropped. Now, before you tell me to fuck myself again, let's talk. You know Troy Berlington, right?"

"Yeah, I know him. He's our local friendly drug dealer, even if he is Elvis. Hey, Elvis was into drugs wasn't he?"

"Not the topic here now Jerry, back to Berlington. What is he up to, why did he murder Max Petrocelli?"

"Petrocelli? Berlington didn't have anything to do with that. Max was stupid and had it set up to pretend he was Elvis to pick up some cutie at the Flamingo the night he was torched. Berlington loaned Max an outfit and his car to go do the deed, but something went wrong, or so Berlington says. Max was killed and Berlington went into hiding. Someone wanted Berlington dead and it was probably his drug rivals. They just got the wrong guy."

"Max and Berlington weren't enemies? Didn't

Berlington have a fling with Max's wife?"

"Sure, but Max didn't care, they were horndog buddies. They liked to play games with the women they picked up during their shows. Max would dress up like Elvis to poke the women in a room they had at the Flamingo Hotel."

"You know anything about the death of Doris Petrocelli?"

"Nope, that one's a mystery to me. Berlington never spoke of it either, but I think Troy was a bit worried when it happened and with Max's death. That's why he was hiding out."

"From who?"

"There's a guy in town who had a foothold here years back for drug running from Arizona to California. The guy disappeared for about two years but now he's back to claim his territory again. Everyone is running scared over this guy, he's a bad ass and is doing away with his competition one by one."

"Do you know who he is?"

"They call him Torch, he likes burning his enemies. That's as much as I know or want to know. Three burnings in the last week alone I heard. Max and two pushers out in the desert from the word I got."

"So this has nothing to do with Elvis? Have you

ever heard of Charles Lawton?"

"Lawton, yeah, he was a mule for drugs from LA to here. He'd come into town and bring his goodies to Berlington for resale. I heard Lawton was killed too, don't know why but I do know Berlington was scared when he heard that."

"So your take is that this Torch is getting back into the business and is eliminating the competition?"

"Yep, that's about it."

"Any idea on how to find this Torch?"

"He's got men taking care of his business, he don't show his face and from what I hear it's a good thing, the guy is supposed to be ugly."

"Ugly? You mean he doesn't have a pretty face?"

"No, he's really ugly. He even wears a mask, some say his face was removed by a rival dealer. He never let's anyone see him, unless they are going to die. Then he scares the hell out of them before he torches them."

Lynn looked to Deacon and said to go check for any similar cases of torching. Deacon went out and Lynn said. "So Berlington is running scared from Torch and this guy is like the Phantom of Vegas?"

"Hey I like that, the Phantom of Vegas, yeah, that fits."

Lynn thought that Jerry was getting a little too happy about this, "Okay Jerry, calm down. I'll talk to the D.A. but if I have any more questions, you need to be right there with the answers, got it?"

"Sure, just don't say that I told you about Torch, I don't want to be on the end of his matchbook."

Lynn turned and went out of the room, told a uniform to take him to a cell and then she came to observation and sat.

"So any smart remarks about what he said?" she asked.

I was thinking about the possibilities but it couldn't be. "Do you remember Kris Wallace?" I asked.

"Yep, he was toast in the car crash while we chased him out highway 15. What about him?"

"He was a connection for drugs from Arizona to California and it was about two years ago the car exploded and he burnt up. Seems like a coincidence doesn't it?"

"Jim they found his skeleton in the wreckage, he's gone, and he's not our phantom. Yes, this is just a coincidence."

Deacon came back in and sat, "There was a report four days ago of a burn out in the desert off the 15, and when the desert patrol spotter plane sent a car to the location, they found a body, toasted well and unidentifiable. Could be one of the victims Jerry mentioned."

"Great, now we have another psycho running around Vegas scaring up the drug dealers," Lynn said.

"Another vigilante cleaning up our streets from the scum," Trapper said.

"I thought I told you not to speak anymore today," Lynn said.

"You did but I didn't agree to it."

"Damn, I'll have to pay more attention from now on. So we need to find this Torch, I'll have to pull in all my C.I.'s and find out what the word on the street is. Are you two going back to the Elvis convention?" she asked me.

"Not if I can help it. That side is all explained away now, so I can go collect on the case the Elvis people hired me for."

"I get a cut, since it was my brilliant interrogation of the prisoner that broke your case," Lynn said with a laugh.

"Oh come on, he gave that information way too easily. You didn't even have to beat him for it."

Bob Moats

"Criminal's fear me; they know it's useless to hide it from me. I deserve a reward."

"I'll reward you with my undying thanks." I looked to Trapper and said, "Shall we go?"

He stood and I followed him out, turning at the door I said, "I still think it's Kris Wallace."

"Get out before I toast you," she said.

"Well I do," I said to Trapper as we left the building.

"Who is this guy Wallace?"

"Back when Penny and I came out here for her TV convention and the showgirls were turning up dead, he worked for Nick North, took my job when I quit working for North a few years earlier. Turned out he was the mastermind of a drug running business between Kingman, Arizona through Vegas to California. The day we found him he led us on a high speed chase out on the desert highway and he crashed off the side of the road. He stupidly fired his gun with gasoline pouring down around him, blew him and the car sky high. I really would believe Torch was Wallace, but they did find his skeleton in the wreckage. So we have a mystery."

"Are we going to the convention to tell Morgan about our findings?"

"No, I'm done with them today, I'm only interested in going home for now. We have tomorrow to go prove

169

that Wallace is Torch, and settle with the Elvi, plural."

"You really are going to try and prove that aren't you?"

"Well it fits, except for his remains in the burned out Porsche; I'll have to figure that out."

"Porsche? He blew up in a Porsche, that's a crime."

"Yep, a cherry red Porsche owned by Nick North. Too bad he didn't take Nick's Lexus."

We got into my van and I took us back to the house. Trapper said he'd see me in the morning and went to his Jeep parked off the side. I watched him drive off as I heard the front door open, it was Penny.

"About time you got back. We are all partied out and need to get Val and Blake back to their hotel. We need the van to haul all the stuff they bought."

"How did you get it home if you need the van to carry it all?"

"We made a couple trips, it added up."

"Okay let's do it, I'm beat and want to crash for the night."

"I haven't seen you almost all day and you want to crash? I'm offended."

"Okay you have me after we get Lucy and Ricky

back to the MGM."

"Lucy and Ricky? You mean I Love Lucy?"

"Yes dear, they are a strange team. Now go gather your children and their booty and get moving."

We had Val, Blake and all the stuff they bought today in the van and delivered to the hotel. They found a cart and loaded all the goodies on it and went off to play with their toys. I drove us back to the house and in to find Willy had pulled his dry dog food around the kitchen again.

"You take care of your son, I'm going into the bedroom to fall on the bed," I said and walked away.

"Thank you very much, see if I treat you to my delights tonight."

I could hear her as I went into the bedroom and laid down on the bed, it had to be minutes when I was asleep.

I was back in Henderson at Nick North's house by his pool talking to Deacon about him staying in Vegas to live with Lynn. I was happy for him and then I turned to see Kris Wallace standing in the back doorway with the uzi. He led us into the house and then we were suddenly driving very fast on Highway 15 following Wallace in Nick's Porsche when Wallace spunout and turned the car over in the desert. Gasoline was pouring down but he fired the gun and the car blew up in a big ball of flame and car parts.

I stood watching the fire as I saw Wallace crawl out of the flaming car and he was walking towards me, still burning. He got right up to me and held out his flaming hand and grabbed me by the throat as I tried to scream.

I was being shaken by Penny as she was calling to me, I opened my eys and she said, "You and those damn dreams, now what?"

*

Chapter 23

I sat up but was still shaking, Penny sat next to me and took my hand as I said, "I was remembering the day Kris Wallace killed himself in the car crash. He came at me and was strangling me with a flaming hand. Damn, it was as bad as the time I dreamt about being buried alive in the coffin."

"What brought that on?" she asked.

I explained my day and the news about Torch. "So I felt that it was a lot like Wallace was back. But we know he couldn't be, they found his remains in the burned out car. It may be just something that coincides with this incident."

"Jim, don't obsess over this, you've had plenty of criminals to catch, good and bad ones, so find this guy then you can sleep well."

"Good and bad ones? How can a criminal be good?" I asked.

"Good in the sense of really evil. Goodly evil and somewhat bad."

"Ah, I see. I think. Anyways, I do really need to solve this, but I need sleep and that isn't an option right now. Let's go watch a comedy movie on the TV and maybe a little good sex."

"Good sex as in evil, because I can give you evil sex."

I just sat looking at her, then smiled. "Let's just go see what's on TV and open a few beers." I stood and went out.

"Beer will help with the evil sex," she called to me and followed.

We were plopped in front of the jumbo TV mounted on the wall, watching "Castle" on the TiVo, munching chips and enjoying our beer. The show ended and Penny leaned over and gave me a big kiss on the cheek. She didn't mention anything about Wallace, she was always considerate of my fears. Being a senior citizen, I found fears were more prevalent as I grew older. I guess being closer to death made us that way.

"Want to grab a breast?" she said with a smile.

I just sat watching the TV, then without looking at her reached over and caressed her lovely round breast. "Not bad for an old lady," I said.

"Hey, I work out and I take care of my body," she laughed.

"Yes, and I take care of the good parts of your body." I stood and headed to the bedroom, "Are you going to just sit there?"

She followed.

I slept well that night, standard dreams, no sign of Wallace lurking about. Next morning we were up and getting ready for the day. I left my personal bathroom and went out to the kitchen where I found Penny and Angelo slaving over a hot stove.

"What's for breakfast?" I asked.

Penny beamed, "Angelo is teaching me to make crepes, want yours with blueberry or apple?"

"Apple is nice, how long have you been at this?"

"About two hours, and thirty-some crepes later. We may open a store to sell them. Even the burnt ones I made."

Angelo laughed and said, "Mrs. R. just needs a little more practice. She'll do all right."

"Thank you Angelo. Now both of you sit and I will serve breakfast."

The big man and I went to the snack bar and sat

as Penny prepared the plates of food and brought them to us.

"Angelo, does Buck have a new job for you?" I asked as I ate the crepe, it was good. I wasn't sure if Penny made it or Angelo, I wasn't going to ask.

"Yep, he wants me to pick up some celebrity at the airport and escort her around town. I'm not going to mess up like I did with Tandy Messner, I'll will be on guard."

I thought back to Tandy Messner, the porn star who came to town to participate in the big World Porn Film Festival and Awards. Angelo was assigned to protect her but they were kidnapped and Tandy was taken. Trapper and Angelo finally found her and rescued her and all was good. Even for her mob boss father who came to town to find his daughter.

"Angelo, you didn't mess up with Tandy, you just were a victim of an almost perfect kidnapping, but you found her and that's important."

"Thanks, Mr. R., that makes me feel a little better."

"So you just need to be alert and never let your guard down. And don't forget to enjoy yourself."

"I will, thanks," he said and stood. He wolfed down the last bite of crepe on his plate and said he had to go get ready. He left Penny and me in the kitchen as we finished eating our food.

"Okay, these aren't bad at all. I like them; do you

think you can make them again without Angelo being around?"

She gave me a big smile and stood, "I have to get ready for work, duty calls." She left the room and went to off to her bathroom.

I looked down to Willy sitting at my feet licking his chops and looking hungry, and said, "She's not going to be able to make these again is she?"

He yipped and I put my plate down on the floor so he could lick the remains off. I went back to my bathroom and finished getting ready. Penny had gone off to her job taking Willy with her and I was waiting for Trapper to arrive.

About twenty minutes later, the driveway alarm rang and I went to the front door. Trapper came up and I let him in.

"Anything for breakfast?" was the first thing he asked.

I had him sit at the snack bar, took out a plate putting the burnt crepes on it and handed it to him.

"What's this?" he asked.

"Well if you could start your day a little earlier, you would have gotten some decent crepes. So suffer."

He laughed and ate the scorched crepes. "You've never had food my mother cooked. I'm used to this. So what's on the agenda for today?"

176

"I'd like to talk to Joe Lang and see what his take is on the Wallace case. And we need to go tell Morgan that his Elvises are safe now, hopefully."

"You're not going to let the Wallace death die are you?"

"I just want to be sure. I like to cover all bases."

"Jim, you said it yourself, Wallace's remains were found in the car? What more do you want?"

"Proof."

We finished up in the house and were in the van driving to the Clark County Medical Examiner's office and morgue where Joe Lang had his office. We identified ourselves to the desk officer and he called Joe who said to let us in.

I wasn't fond of the morgue, but who would be, all the dead bodies and autopsies going on. It smelled bad and looked worse. Not that the building was unclean, but the blood and guts that they pulled from the bodies made it seem unclean.

When we found him, Joe was cutting into the body of a gangbanger from the looks of the corpse. Good build and lots of tats everywhere on his now dissected body. Joe looked up and smiled behind the plastic faceplate protecting him from bodily waste splats.

"Hey Jim, Will, what's up?" he greeted us.

Blue Suede Murders

"When you aren't elbow deep in the inside of your victim, I'd like to talk to you about a former autopsy," I said.

"No problem," he said and turned to his assistant and said, "Finish up will you, Dave?"

Dave took over the gruesome task as Joe led us to his office after throwing his scrubs into a container. We sat in the modest office as Joe sat at his desk, "What's up?"

"Do you remember a case two years back. A death by explosion of a car out on Highway 15. Kris Wallace?"

Joe turned to his computer and did a quick type on the keyboard and read what was on the screen.

"Sure, the Porsche flame out, drug cartel leader died in the explosion, what do you need to know?"

"Did you have enough evidence to confirm the body was Wallace?"

Joe read a bit more of the report on his monitor, then said, "Well, there were skeletal remains in the car, he was the only person in the vehicle from the police reports, so we assumed it was him. There wasn't much to identify the body, Wallace had no priors or dental on record and the body was pretty much burnt up in the fire, it was a hot one. Why? You think it may not be him, how's that possible?"

"I don't know Joe, just a gut feeling. I can't explain the remains, maybe I'm wrong and it was Wallace."

"Sometimes gut feelings can be just gas," Joe said with a big grin.

"You're a big help."

"Sorry but that was the determination of Wallace's death, now stop obsessing over it."

"Damn you sound like my wife," I said with a smile.

"Well you should listen to her, now you need to find your real killer, and get back on track."

"Thanks Joe, I'll be in touch."

We said our good-byes and left. Out in the van, I sat. Trapper asked, "You still thinking about Wallace?"

"No, I'm trying to put someone else in this scenario. Do you know anyone in the drug trade who we can talk to?"

"Me, know anyone who deals drugs? Are you saying I know law breakers?"

"Just what I'm asking, who can we talk to about this Torch, who may not be afraid to talk?"

"Well I may know one bad ass who isn't intimidated by anyone, but it may cost you."

"Let's go," I said and started the van.

*

Chapter 24

I followed Trapper's direction up to north Vegas, into the seedier part of town. He pointed to a building and said to park in front.

"Is my van going to be safe out here, I'm not wanting to come out and find it stolen?" I said.

"It'll be safe, besides we can see it from the front window of the building. Lionel likes to see the street out front for any cops sneaking up on him."

"We aren't going to be caught in a raid are we?"

Trapper laughed and said, "We're safe." He got out and we went to the front of the building where I saw a small sign over the front door. It read, "Welcome to Reverend Lionel's House of Redemption."

"Is this some kind of a church?" I asked as we reached the door.

"It's an outreach and rehab center for drug addicts and other such people."

"Other such people? What's that mean?"

"Dealers and mules who want to get out of the life. The good Reverend is a former Vegas cop who has a lot of power in town. He doesn't take shit from anyone, as they say."

We entered and I heard a deep booming voice from across the room, "Will Trapper, you old reprobate you. What you doin' here?"

"Lionel, I had hoped never to see you again, but I'm in need of some info."

We walked to the back of the room where the big man sat at a desk. He was black as the bottom of a coal mine, and had pure white teeth and eyes that were bright with his extra wide smile. He stood as we approached and I was surprised to see he had to be at least six foot three or four. He must have weighed in at around three hundred pounds, but not flab, all muscles. He came around the desk extended his hand to Trapper and then pulled him into a hug.

Trapper introduced me to Reverend Lionel Jeffers. The powerful looking man smiled, shook my hand, thankfully no hug, and asked us to sit. I sat on a chair that luckily faced the window where I could see my van. Trapper started the conversation.

"Lionel, we need some information about a new dealer in town, he goes by the nickname Torch. You know anything about him?"

The big man stopped smiling, "Whatcha want to know for?"

Blue Suede Murders

"We suspect he may be murdering other dealers and we need to find him. Is this a problem?"

"Honestly, I'd like him off the streets too, he's a bad one, pure evil. I heard he tortured a kid, barely eighteen for taking some drugs that he didn't pay for. Don't know the circumstances but the kid was barely alive when my men found him. He didn't know where this Torch was at, they had him blindfolded."

"They let him go alive?" I asked.

"As a warning to anyone else who thinks about stealing from him, just a warning. I suspect the next person won't be so lucky."

"Anyone know where to find him or where he comes from?" Trapper asked.

"Don't know where he is at, but he's originally from here, or so I hear. The man is totally nameless, no identifying background and no story. My followers have just been avoiding him. I got three pushers in this week looking to get out of the drug trade because of him. They's all running scared. Sorry I don't have more for you."

"Thanks Lionel, if you hear anything, call me," Trapper said as he handed him a card.

"So you've gone private, eh?"

"Yep, got tired of the cop business, all the hassles and red tape from the brass. I'm working with my friend Jim here, we have a nice new office over on

Industrial and Flamingo, you should come for a visit. So how's the savior business doing?"

Jeffers gave out a healthy laugh and said, "That's cute, I save people but I don't walk on water. I leave that to those more experienced. I have a good flock, many substance abusers who can't keep up with the high cost of being high. They realize that they have a problem and I provide counseling and referrals for professional help. It keeps me busy and helps people who want it."

"Did you ever hear of Troy Berlington?" I asked.

"Elvis? Sure, so he was one of the reasons I get people in here? I had no proof, just speculation from the street people that there was an Elvis dealing drugs. I didn't know which one, but your question is a one plus one, now I definitely know. I read where he was burned up in his caddie."

"Nope, that was Max Petrocelli, Dean Martin impersonator who wanted to be Elvis for a night. Troy is still alive and running scared himself from Torch. If we find Berlington, maybe we'll find Torch."

"Well, I will ask around and see if we can find Troy and give you a call."

"You have a good network of underworld figures, I'm surprised you don't have a fix on Torch already."

"As I said, Torch is a figure to be reckoned with. He has everyone on their toes."

Blue Suede Murders

Trapper turn to me and said, "Well, we need to go talk to a head Elvis now."

We stood and then Trapper said to me, "Jim, this place runs on donations, you hold the purse strings; think we can contribute to the good Reverend's cause."

I had to grin and took out my checkbook, "You are sneaky Will." I made out the check for a good sum and handed it to the Reverend.

"Thank you so much Mr. Richards. I've read about your exploits in fighting crime in the city. You do good work."

I thanked him, we said our good-byes and left.

In the van Trapper sat back, smiled and said, "I warned you it would cost."

"It's a good cause, I don't mind. It's also deductable." I smiled back to him and started the van.

We were back in the MGM Grand and looking for Morgan. We found him in the exhibition hall at the booth for the competition. He was adding names to the board of winners in their categories. I called to him and he came over.

"Mr. Richards, you have anything for me?"

"We've now determined that the Elvises are no longer in danger. The death of Berlington and Lawton were related to drug dealings. The only problem is

Berlington isn't dead. The body in the caddie was Max Petrocelli and Berlington is still on the loose. But he's no threat to your people now. Berlington isn't interested in the convention now, he's running from a dangerous man. Someone called Torch," I said and noticed that Morgan looked a little shook when I said the name. "Do you know this person?"

"Who, oh, no I've never heard of him. Berlington is still alive? Do you know where he is?"

"No, we're looking for him and this guy Torch. Would be nice if we had some information to catch both of them. You wouldn't know anything about this would you?"

He was acting distracted and then said, "No, I don't know anything about this, but I'll check around and see what I can find out. I'm sorry but I have to go get ready for the last awards ceremony." He went off quickly.

"Do you think he was acting strange?" Trapper said with a smirk.

"For a middle aged guy dressed like Elvis, no, nothing strange about him."

"So where to now?"

"Let's go back to the office, I want to talk to Angelo and see what Earl's up to."

"Sounds like a plan." Trapper smiled.

Blue Suede Murders

We drove out to our building and in to find Buck in the lobby where Lacey should be.

"What's going on?" I asked.

"Lacey is at the DMV getting her driver's license renewed," he said.

"Are you kidding, that will take all day, maybe into tomorrow. The DMV in Vegas is a public hell," I said. "She could have hired one of those people who sit for you all day."

"Not for her license renewal, they have to take your picture."

"Oh well, have fun being a secretary," I said and went to Earl's office with Trapper following. We got there and he was sitting at this desk reading some papers.

He looked up, saw us and said "Don't even come in here needing help with missing brides or grooms, I finally found the errant groom, drunk in a hooker's apartment. I couldn't believe it, a three day drunk. He had some serious issues with getting married. I returned him to his bride but I don't think she wants him back. Now what do you want?"

"I need some intel from your black ops friends, we have a local drug kingpin who needs to be put out of business. Think you know anyone who can help?"

"What's the mug's name?"

"No name, just a handle, Torch. He's from Vegas originally, something happened to his face about two years ago, so he now wears a mask. Frightens his victims before he burns then up."

"Does this have something to do with the Elvis in the Cadillac bonfire?"

"We have it from an unreliable source it is the same."

"Unreliable?"

"He's a hood, so we're taking it with a grain of salt. And the Elvis who was in the car wasn't the person we thought it was. Torch hit the wrong man, just for being in the wrong place at the wrong time. The real Elvis impersonator is on the run."

"So you're saying Elvis is still in the building?"

*

Chapter 25

"Berlington, for some reason, is hiding out from Torch, or so we think. That's all we have so far. If you can come up with anything it would help," I said.

"Mystery drug czar, with mutilated face and terrorizing the city, my cup of tea. I'll see what I can find," Earl said with a big grin.

"Now that I've covered the black Ops people, I need to go talk to the mob people."

"Covering all bases on this one, eh?" Earl said.

"Yep, is Angelo around?"

"Haven't seen him, I heard from our cute new bald-headed receptionist that he was out on a protection detail. Ask Buck."

"I'll tell him you think he's cute," I said as Trapper and I went out. Back in the lobby, Buck was trying to answer the phones, but it kept ringing and no matter which button he pushed it didn't answer.

"Why don't you just pick up the receiver?" I asked.

"Jimmy, this is a new fancy-schmancy operating system Lacey has, not just some phone." He picked up the receiver and said hello. He smiled and said to hold on and handed the thing to me.

I gave him a smirk, "Hello, Jim Richards speaking."

There was a brief silence, then I heard a raspy voice say, "Richards, keep your nose out of my business or I'll burn you good."

"Who is this?" I asked.

"Someone you don't want to mess with, now back off." The voice stopped and the phone disconnected.

I turned to Trapper and said, "I think I just talked to the Torch. He's not a friendly guy. I think we all need to be on alert now." I turned to Buck, "Be sure to carry your .38 at all times around the office, I'll explain later. If you see a person wearing a mask come in, shoot first, talk later." I handed the phone back to Buck and asked, "Is Angelo around or close by?"

"Angelo is escorting an actress while she does a photo shoot at the Venetian. He should be done in about an hour," Buck said.

"Have him talk to me or if I'm not here, call when he gets in."

I went to my office, Trapper said he had some calls to make and went to his office. I sat at my desk and picked up my desk phone. I called Lynn.

When she answered I spoke, "Hey, I just got a call from someone who I think was Torch, he threatened me. I don't like being threatened."

"Did you do a reverse call back or see the caller ID?" she asked.

Duh, I didn't think about that. "No, we have this new phone system and I don't know how it works yet," I said as an excuse.

"Can't Lacey show you?"

"She's at the DMV today renewing her license."

"Poor girl, let me know if you don't see her within forty-eight hours and I'll send backup in. Torch didn't identify himself?"

"No, he just threatened me to keep my nose out and back off or he'll burn me good, I just assumed it was him."

"I haven't found out anything from my informants, the word on the street is mum. No one wants to talk about it. Hey, how did he even know you had your nose in it?

"I was thinking on that. Do you know Reverend Lionel Jeffers?"

"Lionel? Sure, he's a good guy, ex-cop gone to religion and helping the street people. Why?"

"Trapper and I talked to him earlier and he said he'd check on Torch, but I'm thinking my second contact with someone may be the person who ratted me out to Torch. An Elvis turned me in, I'm figuring."

"Who, shall we question him?"

"Morgan Taylor, you've met him and spoke with him when Lawton was killed. Trapper and I talked to him after the Reverend and he was acting strange when I mentioned Torch, and that Berlington was still alive. Maybe we do need to talk to him again."

"Shall we meet at the convention center and beat on him a while?"

"I'll meet you there in a half hour. Thanks," I said and hung up. I went to Trapper's office and he was going through his drawers. "Looking for the bodies?"

"Looking for my handcuffs. I was sure I had them in this drawer."

"Maybe you took them home to use on Samantha?"

"We've been cooling our relationship; no I didn't use them on her. Oh, I know, they're in my car. I put them there when I thought I had a date with Lori, a waitress I met the other night."

"You had plans for the cuffs?"

"Always good to be prepared. What do you want?"

"I'm going back to the MGM to have a heart to heart with Morgan, want to come?"

"Thanks, no, I'm fed up with Elvises, go have fun and call if you really need me."

"Fine, don't back me up, I'll remember that." I left his office and went back to the lobby. I was surprised to see Lacey, she jumped a little bit when I came out.

"I was waiting for you to spring out on me. I am about up to here with the DMV and all the thousands of people camping out in the place trying to get service."

"How did you get out so early?"

Blue Suede Murders

"I started to get in the line this morning at five and waited three hours to get in and got a low number. By noon there had to be over five hundred people there, it was a circus. I was number twenty in line and still had to wait for hours from the time I got in. They should destroy that place."

"Glad you survived, Lynn had the police on call if you didn't come back."

"Thank her for me. This is the last day for the Elvis convention isn't it?"

"Yep and I'm going back there right now to do one more thing before I'm through with the Elvi, plural. So just letting you know where I'll be."

"Go play, I'm going to try and undo the mess Buck made of the phone system, all the buttons are reprogrammed."

"Have fun," I said and went to Buck's office. "Tell Angelo to call me when he gets in, I'm going to the MGM Grand again and will be back later."

Twenty minutes later, I entered the convention center and saw Lynn standing by the sign-in table with Deacon. I came up and said, "Have you seen him?"

"No and I talked to some fat guy in a tight Elvis jumpsuit costume saying he put another man in charge for the rest of the day and took off. I'm now wondering if he's in on this."

"He was on stage when Lawton was shot. Did they do GSR on him?" I asked.

"I'd have to check, but he could have been wearing gloves. Do you know where Morgan lives?"

"No, should I? Let's find out from someone in the convention committee."

We went into the convention hall and found a couple Elvi who were talking. Lynn flashed her badge and asked if they knew where Morgan lived. One man pulled out his phone, checked his contacts and gave us an address. The three of us went out to the parking lot and I said I'd follow them over.

"No, I want a ride in this van of yours, I hear it's sweet," Lynn said.

"Sure, if you don't mind leaving your car here."

"No I have my own car today. Motor pool didn't have any good cars."

I was just going to lead them to the van when I heard my name called, it was Blake.

"Hey Blake, why are you alone?" I asked as he came running up.

"Ah said ah wanted to go explore the strip alone, so Penny took Val to her studio for the show. Ah've been wandering for a couple hours and was just going back to the room when ah saw you."

"Well, you're more than welcome to join us. We're going to question a suspect. I'll explain on the way." We went to my van and everyone climbed in. Lynn had the address and I steered in that direction.

"I must say this is nice and comfy, so you came all the way across the country in it from your book tour?" Lynn asked.

"Yep, it was very handy and comfortable. Penny and I plan to use it more for camping in the future, now that she is getting used to camping."

"Brave girl. So the only person who could have informed Torch about you being involved in his business was Morgan?"

"It's the only possibility. Unless he talked to someone else after I talked to him and they told Torch. It was just so quick from the time I talked to Morgan and Torch's call. Too quick to be someone else though."

"Hopefully we can get Morgan to talk," Lynn said.

"Blake how was your exploring the strip?" I asked him.

"Good, ah got a laugh out of those people who hand out the flyers for the escort women, is that legal?"

Lynn laughed and said, "It's legal to hand out the flyers but it's a grey area for the escorts. They get away with it though."

"That wouldn't fly back in ma hometown of Palatka."

"No offense, but very little flies in Palatka." I said with a smile.

We arrived at the apartment of Morgan and went to his door but found it partially open. Lynn and Deacon drew their weapons and told Blake and me to wait outside. I stood by the door with my hand on my Glock, listening. I could see the two of them quietly walking around the place. They disappeared down a hallway and I suddenly heard a gunshot, then it was quiet again.

I pulled my Glock and Blake followed me in. I called for Lynn and she yelled that they were in the bedroom. We went in and found Morgan on the floor, alive but soaked in what smelled like gasoline. There was another man by the wall dead from a gunshot wound.

"It's not Torch, but I think we are getting close now."

*

Chapter 26

"So Torch sent one of his men to do the job? He's too busy to appear himself?" I asked.

"Once we get Morgan cleaned up from the gas and woke up, maybe he'll be more willing to talk about the man who wanted him dead," Lynn said.

I was looking at the dead man and asked, "I presume he pointed a gun for you to shoot him?"

"Gee, I guess that's why you're the private eye. Yes, when we came into the room, he had a lighter in his hand and then went for his gun when he saw us. He brought it up and Deacon fired," Lynn said.

"I gave him a chance to give up, but he raised it and gave me no choice, so I fired. Now I'll have to do all that paperwork because I had a deadly shooting. Damn," Deacon said with a groan.

"It was you or him; at least a little paperwork won't kill you," I said.

Lynn said, "I called CSI and Joe Lang, as soon as he went down, they should be here soon to record the scene. For the record of the shoot."

I took Blake and we went back out to the rest of Morgan's apartment and snooped around for a while until Joe Lang popped in.

"Hey Jim, what's up?" he said with a smile.

"You have a body in the back bedroom, shot by Deacon in self-defense."

"Thanks, I'll get on it right away then." He went to the back room followed by two EMS techs who were going to take Morgan out. He was still stinking from the liquid sprayed to set him on fire and he was lucky to be alive.

CSI came in, so Blake and I went outside of the apartment to let them do their forensic investigation. It wasn't like what you see on TV, they didn't do the same intensive exam of the place like their counterparts on the shows did. Real life isn't all that TV real.

Lynn came out leaving Deacon to go over his statement as to the shooting. It was sad that police have to be under such scrutiny when a perp is shot. The police have to cover their asses for every little detail or end up with a ton of lawsuits by the victim's family. There should be no rights for crime, no lawsuits or pleas, but this world isn't fair all the time, even for the bad guys.

"Once Morgan is ready to talk, we may have more to go on."

"I'd suggest putting a couple guards on Morgan, just in case Torch tries again," I said.

"Yea, I had that thought too. No sense losing him now that we have him. The med tech said he had a concussion but would probably be all right in a short while. This Torch doesn't fool around."

My cellphone buzzed and I excused myself from Blake and Lynn and went to answer it. I saw it was Angelo by the caller ID, I answered.

"Angelo, how's your job going so far?"

"I like it real well, it's not like breaking a few legs for the family, but I get to protect some good people. I like it."

"I'm glad you're happy. Now I have a problem you may be able to help with. I got a drug kingpin who needs to be stopped. I know don Traviano didn't tolerate drug running in his family, but maybe you can do a little checking with the other families to find out something about this guy?"

"Be more than happy to Mr. R., just give me the mook's name and I'll see what we got."

"All we know is his moniker, they call him Torch. He's from Vegas originally but may have moved away for a couple years, but he's back now and burning people to death, in addition to drug running. See if that rings a bell with anyone."

"Will do Mr. R., I'll get back to you as soon as possible."

I thanked him and hung up. I turned to Lynn who was listening in on my conversation. She smiled and said, "You enjoy getting the mob involved in your investigations don't you?"

"On this case it's necessary, I also included the black ops people; Earl is putting in a call to his buddies to see what they have. I hope we can get some background on him."

"You don't still think it's Wallace do you?"

"No, the evidence it against it. Just a coincidence of similarities. I'm pretty sure it can't be him. I stood there and watched as he was blown to bits by the explosion, no one could have walked away from that mess."

"And they did have the skeleton." Lynn added.

"Yes, they did have that too. Blake, shall we go see what the women are up to?" I asked the young man taking all this excitement in.

"Shore, ah'm ready to git going. This is more than ah kin handle for one day."

Lynn and I both chuckle at the simplicity of the young cop from Florida who, in a matter of days, would be getting married.

I turned to Lynn, "When you get Morgan ready to talk, I'd like to be there."

Blue Suede Murders

"I'll call you," she said.

"Can you get a ride back to your car?" I asked.

"No problem, I have enough rank to get any car I want to take us," she said with a big grin and went back into the apartment.

I took Blake to the van and we drove back to the office. Penny and Val were in the lobby with Lacey as they were examining and playing the new phone system computer.

"Doesn't take much to amuse you does it?" I asked Penny.

"Yes, I find you so amusing and simple," she said as she leaned over the counter to give me a kiss.

I turned to Blake and asked if he was hungry, he said he was so I turned to Penny and said, "I had a thought."

She didn't even blink and replied, "Prove it."

I was a bit thrown off by that, but continued, "What say we all go to Bistro's for a nice dinner?"

Penny picked up her purse, grabbed Willy who was sleeping on Lacey's desk and said, "I'm ready."

We had a nice meal at our favorite restaurant and then took a ride up the strip. Blake was in the front passenger captain's chair watching all the people walking around the bright shiny casinos and hotels.

Val and Penny were seated behind us talking wedding stuff and I could see Blake wince every now and then.

I dropped Blake, Val and Penny back at the office and said, "I have to go interrogate a bad guy, I'll catch up to you later."

"I'll probably take Val and Blake back to the house and have some snacks, if you want some, don't take all day."

"I'll be along as soon as possible." I left and drove back to Metro.

Lynn and Deacon were talking to Weber as I entered the squad room. Weber saw me and waved me over.

"Jim, how did you enjoy the Elvis convention?" Weber asked.

"I found it interesting, and entertaining. Did you enjoy it?" I said figuring he knew that I was with Trapper when he took the pictures of Weber in costume.

"Since my secret is out, yes I enjoyed the convention and in case you wondered why I was dressed as an Elvis, I'm part of the Flying Elvis' Parasail Team."

"You actually jump out of a plane and fall to the earth yelling Hunka-hunka?" I said, now amazed.

He laughed and said, "Well, hopefully I don't fall but yes, I jump out of a plane. I was a combat ranger in the war. Jumped hundreds of times, loved it. Well, not jumping into a combat zone but just the rush of watching the earth fly up to you."

"Captain, I have a new respect for you," I said.

He turned to Lynn, "Well go find out what you can about this Torch, get it closed up." He walked off leaving us with a different opinion of the man.

"Sometimes he amazes me," Deacon said. "He's a frightening little man."

Lynn laughed and said, "You're a frightening big man, so don't judge."

"Is Morgan ready?" I asked.

"Yep, he's been cleaned up and given enough pills to keep him awake for days. I got him sitting in room three waiting."

"What's your plan of attack on him?"

"I got the rubber hose ready; otherwise I'll just sweet talk him." Lynn went off leaving Deacon and I alone.

"Are you and Lynn getting along better?" I asked.

"We had a good talk last night, we both have been on edge working and living together, it's not easy. So we set down some ground rules for bringing work home, or we will have to separate jobs. I could go to vice, but I don't think Lynn would like me in contact with the hookers all day," he said with a grin.

Lynn yelled from down the hall if we were coming. We followed the call. She was standing outside room three watching Morgan squirming in his chair, dressed in an orange jumpsuit they usually give to prisoners. He looked all scrubbed and clean.

"We should have burned his clothing, wouldn't have been hard with all the fuel on it, but CSI bagged it for evidence. Shall we begin?" she said as she went into the room, Deacon followed her and I went to observation and sat. Too bad they don't have popcorn in here.

*

Chapter 27

"Morgan, we meet again, how's the convention doing?" Lynn asked.

"It was doing fine until today," he said with a frown.

"Okay Morgan, we don't have anything to charge you with so far, other than accessory, so you can relax. Maybe I'll see if I can get those charges dropped for your cooperation. How's that sound?"

Blue Suede Murders

He didn't say anything.

"Morgan, we can release you and maybe Torch will do the job of killing you himself this time. Now do you want to help us stop this maniac?"

He looked at Lynn then Deacon, "Do you think you can really protect me? This guy is not normal, he thrives on burning people. I heard he was burned badly years ago and he's always in pain over it, so he wants other people to suffer too."

"We can protect you Morgan, by putting him away. Help us find him. What do you know?"

He was looking around the room as Lynn gave him the time.

"I don't know where he hides out, he moves around from what I understand. I wanted to get on his good side by telling him that the police were closing in on him. Then Torch sent that weasel to my apartment and we had a bit of a fight before he coldcocked me. I didn't know what had happened after that until the paramedics woke me. I can't believe he would kill someone who was trying to help. Son of a bitch."

"Good attitude Morgan, now help us. How did you contact him?"

"I had a number that I got from a pusher I bought my stuff from, yeah, I'm an addict. This pusher said that Torch was looking for someone to fill Berlington's shoes as a dealer for this area of Vegas. Torch's got hooks into a big portion of Clark County and wants to expand down south towards Bullhead City. I said I was interested in taking Berlington's place and the guy gave me a contact number. I didn't use it till earlier today when I called to give him a warning about the cops closing in. I guess Torch didn't like me using his personal number."

"Do you still have the number?"

"It was in my wallet," he said. Lynn looked to Deacon and he went out to get the wallet.

"Do you know anything more about Torch's operation?" Lynn asked.

"Nope, just that he's crazy and wants to rid Vegas of all his competitors. He'll burn the city down if he has to."

"What do you know about Lawton's shooting?"

Morgan started to squirm slightly, sucking on his lower lip and he was avoiding looking at Lynn.

She said again, "Morgan, what do you know about Lawton's shooting?"

"Nothing," he said.

"Morgan, did you shoot Lawton?" she said playing a hunch.

Morgan was sucking air now, looking like he was going to hyperventilate. He was rocking slowly back and forth and his eyes were twitching.

205

Blue Suede Murders

"Morgan, are you all right?" Lynn asked.

"NO! I'm not alright. I did a bad thing, okay! I figured Torch wanted the competition out of the way, so I shot Lawton. He was a runner and was dealing for Berlington. I called Torch today to tell him about you people nosing around and then he asked who the hell was I, so I told him I was the one who shot Lawton, just to get on his good side. The bastard didn't even thank me, he just asked who I was again and I told him. He just hung up on me, then a half hour later that hood shows up and tries to whack me. Son of a bitch!"

"Well, this changes things a bit. Morgan, just sit tight while I go check on a few things." She stood and left the room.

I was watching Morgan still squirming in his chair, then he stood and ran full out towards the glass window of the room looking out to the squad room. His head rammed the glass as it exploded into shards and then he fell down on the jagged pieces still embedded in the frame. His throat caught the glass spikes and he started bleeding profusely. I jumped up and ran out of observation just as Lynn had turned back to see the bloody scene. She yelled for Warren to get an EMS and we pulled him up off the glass.

Deacon was just returning from where he was getting the wallet and ran to us. We had Morgan on the ground and Lynn was applying pressure on the gaping cut in his neck pumping blood. She held her hands there until paramedics rushed in and took over. We stood back and watched.

"I guess he had a guilty streak. Poor bastard," I said.

The paramedics had Morgan bandaged up and on a gurney being taken out. Lynn had called custodial to clean up the mess.

"Why wasn't he handcuffed to the table?" Weber demanded as we later stood watching custodial and the crime scene clean-up people carefully cleaning the area of the blood. Lynn had done a thorough scrubbing of her hands and was now facing Captain Weber.

"He wasn't under arrest; he was a material witness to a crime, his own attempted murder. I questioned him about the shooting of Charles Lawton at the convention and he broke down and confessed to it. I went out to get the file on the Lawton shooting and that's when he went berserk and tried to kill himself. It happened so fast."

Weber looked to me, I said, "I watched it from observation, there was nothing anyone could have done to prevent it."

"Well, do you have anything to go on now?" he said to Lynn.

"We have a phone number of this Torch; we hope it will lead to finding him. Now we can close the case on Lawton at least."

"I want this Torch person in custody ASAP. Get on it," he said and went off.

Blue Suede Murders

We went back to Lynn's office and sat trying to get our nerves back from the incident.

"I watched him just go straight into that window, then it was like he knew, he fell on the glass trying to cut his throat. I guess he thought it would be quick," I said.

"Well, the paramedic said he would probably make it, not good for him, now we know he killed Lawton," Deacon said.

"He was on the stage, all he had to do was go to the curtains and shoot then he rushed out to cover his crime," I said.

Lynn was looking at Morgan's wallet and then opened it. She pulled out a number of cards and a little cash. Sorting through the papers she found one with a phone number on it. She stared at the number then reached to her desk phone and made a call to the electronic investigation division.

"Mike, this is Lynn Carter, can you get a fix on a phone number for me?" she asked then listened. She gave the person the number and thanked him, hanging up. "He'll call me back with the info, all we can do is wait now."

My cell phone buzzed and I pulled it from my pocket. Caller ID said it was Angelo. I stood excusing myself and went out of Lynn's office to the squad room. I answered.

"Angelo, you have anything for me?" I asked.

"I got some information that may help. Seems this Torch guy has no history that I can find, he just came out of nowhere six months ago and started to put an army together. He's got a few California families upset with him, he's muscling in on their supply lines. He got some pull in Columbia for their shipments north and cutting off the wrong people. He's a killing machine from my sources. He's murdered a good number of dealers to grab their territories, burned all of them. He has smugglers in his pocket now and bringing in equipment to set up a meth lab somewhere in Vegas, a big one from the info I got. I did have one source say they think the building is somewhere over around Tropicana and Jones Boulevard in an industrial complex now owned by Torch under the name Deano Hernandez. You probably could try and get the location through your police sources from the name." Angelo took a breath.

"Thank you my friend and thank your friends for me."

"Some of the families I contacted were cooperative, but not friendly, we are on the opposite sides of the life. But they wanted this Torch guy took down, so they gave me as much as they knew," he said and went quiet.

"Well it helps, talk later."

We finished and I hung up. Deano Hernandez? That name was familiar but I couldn't recall it. I went back to Lynn and Deacon as they were sitting waiting for the phone to ring.

"I got something for you if you're real nice to me."

"Does this have anything to do with your mob connections?" Lynn asked.

"If it helps catch Torch, do you care?"

"I guess not. What do you have?"

I told her what Angelo said and she scribbled on a pad in front of her. She was just reaching for her phone when it rang. She answered and listened, then said, "I have some more checking you can do for me. A name, Deano Hernandez. He is supposed to own property around Trop and Jones, can you check county clerks and see if they have an address?" She listened then said, "Thanks." She hung up and looked to Deacon and me.

"Got a good one for you, the phone number was registered to the home of Troy Berlington."

*

Chapter 28

Lynn yelled out to Warren to gather a team to go to Berlington's house again.

"Is Berlington back home now?" Warren asked.

"Don't know, we'll find out," she replied and then said to Deacon and me, "Okay, this isn't making sense, is Torch using Berlington's house now or is Berlington involved with Torch?"

"Well, we just need to do a little raid on the place again to see," Deacon said.

"I suppose since the place is a closed crime scene and the police don't figure they need it any more, what better place to hide out?" I said.

"Could be, we shall see," Lynn said as she stood and headed out followed by Deacon and me. They went to the motor pool to get a car and I went to my van. I followed them back down to Henderson again and to the same gated community. We pulled up to the gate and Lynn stopped to talk to the gate guard. I parked behind them and got out as Lynn was standing by the shack waiting for the guard to get off the phone call he was on. He finished and turned to Lynn and asked how he could help.

"Since we did our attack on Berlington's house, have there been any others coming in for the place?" Lynn asked the guard.

"Sure, some guy named Mr. Hernandez took over the house and has been moving his stuff in," the guard said with a smile.

"Have you seen this Mr. Hernandez?"

"I seen him just this morning when he came to start moving in."

"What's he look like?"

"Not really anything unusual about him, he looks Mexican, short, dark hair and mustache. Not a great looker, but just average."

"When was the last time Mr. Hernandez went in?"

The guard looked at his book and said, "This morning, but he's gone off again."

"Is there anyone else in the house now?"

"Oh sure, Mr. Hernandez has had lots of visitors. Hollywood types who are going to make TV films out here. They're using the house as a base of operations from what I hear. They've had a few trucks pulling in to deliver stuff."

"Okay, we're going in. Don't even call the house to say we're here, understand?" she said as soon as more patrol cars approached, followed by the SWAT van.

Everyone went back to their vehicles and the guard opened the gate. We drove in and I parked away from the official cars and watched them rush the house. I waited by my van until I heard there was a call that the house was under control.

I went up and saw a number of people being brought out of the house by the officers and told to line up on the driveway. Lynn and Deacon were still in the house; I went up to the front door, looking in and could see them talking to another uniform. I slipped inside around the door and into the living room. It was filled with open boxes that contained weapons of all types. Guns, assault rifles and a couple bazookas and a number of flame throwers. Heavy hitting stuff. This guy was expecting trouble.

Deacon came up to me and said, "From what anyone is saying, Torch is not here and they aren't saying where he is. Lynn finally got a call from Mike with the info about the Hernandez warehouse, took a while to get the information from the county clerk. They aren't real friendly when asked to sort through the thousands of property deeds."

"Isn't that stuff all on computer?" I asked.

"Yes it is, but the clerk's office doesn't like to be disturbed," he said with a grin. "Weber finally gave a call into the mayor and he got the clerks moving. As soon as we button up this place, we're heading to the warehouse."

I stood back and watched them put everyone on a short bus called in to take the twelve people to Metro for interrogation and or booking.

Lynn's cell phone rang and she answered it. She listen and then hung up. She called Deacon over and I followed. "It seems Torch must have been called about our little raid, so he called the precinct and wanted to speak to the officer in charge of the raid. The dispatcher told the person who I was, and he wanted to talk to me. The dispatcher said she couldn't transfer the call to my cell phone and asked for his number. He refused and said to tell me I'm on Torch's short list. Gee, I better wear my flame proof outfit now."

"I'm sure you aren't racking up points with him but at least he's aware we aren't fooling around," Deacon said.

"The son of a bitch can rot in hell before he even gets close to me," she smiled.

"At least you'll know who to look for, the guy in the mask," I said.

An officer came up and said they had the prisoners all secure and CSI was in to catalog everything.

Lynn said to gather up any officers who weren't involved in further investigations and get SWAT together, we had another run. He went off as Lynn went to the head CSI and said we were leaving. She'd leave a couple officers to protect them in case any of Torch's men show up.

We went back out to the driveway where Lynn had everyone assembled to give instructions for the next raid.

I stood looking at the house remembering the time we raided Nick North's house, looking for Kris Wallace, who I had to accept died in the car explosion. Nick was still in prison for his connection to the same kind of drug cartel we were fighting today. I could see Wallace doing this, maybe Torch was channeling Wallace from the grave. Okay, I was still believing Torch was Wallace. How I don't know. But it was just a feeling.

Lynn was yelling for everyone to mount up and follow her to the next destination. I got in my van and drove out behind the SWAT van driving back up to Tropicana then over to South Jones Boulevard.

It didn't take long to find the building, it was in the middle of a huge warehouse complex but it was the biggest building. Everyone rolled up to the front and a couple cars drove around the back. The SWAT team all flew out of the van and up to the building. There was a number of cars parked around the front of the building, most were expensive foreign cars, the kind drug dealers would own, or pimps.

Lynn got the call that the warrant was on the way and it was good to go. She yelled to the SWAT Captain to go and they tried to enter but the door was locked. The door ram was brought up and slammed the door open. Everyone flew in and spread out through the offices up front. One room had three men sitting around a table with a pile of cash and machines to count the money. They were taken by surprise and barely had time to draw their weapons before SWAT had them subdued.

Lynn and Deacon went down a hallway and found a door with the word 'Private' stenciled on it. I was back aways with my Glock in hand just in case. They opened the door and went in low. There was gun fire and a couple more uniforms flew by me heading to the door going in with guns up. I went to the door, looked around the edge and saw three more men on the ground, I didn't know if they were shot or surrendered.

Blue Suede Murders

The room was filled with tables and equipment to process meth, I was used to the sight by now having been exposed many times to them following Lynn and Deacon. I was surprised the room didn't blow when there was gun fire. Just lucky I guess.

The building was declared secure and everyone was rounded up. No sight of Torch.

"This sucks," Lynn spit. "We have raided his lairs and haven't found him, where the hell is he?"

She went to one of the men in the money counting room and got in his face. "Talk to me butt breath, where is Torch!" He stood silently, "Talk now or I'll take you into the math lab and set fire to you! You can join Torch with a blown off face."

"Lady it's either you burning me or Torch, but he makes you suffer first. I'm not talking," he said then shut up.

Lynn was not happy, she was fuming, but couldn't do much to the man standing before her. She suddenly turned and gave the man a swift kick to his balls and he went down screaming.

She bent down and said, "I can make you suffer too, asshole."

All the men were carted off and another CSI team was in to secure the scene. The bomb squad was called in to dismantle the meth lab and we were standing outside the building when a truck pulled into the drive. It got up to us before the driver realized what was going on and tried to drive back out.

Deacon jumped on the cab running board and reached in the open window, pulling the driver's head down. He pulled the door open and rammed the shift into park causing the truck to grind to a stop. Deacon pulled the man out of the cab and got him on the ground. Lynn called a couple uniforms over and told them to watch the driver as she and Deacon went to the back of the truck, followed by me.

Deacon pulled up the rolling door of the cargo area and we found a whole lot of bags and boxes of drugs, and ingredients ready for processing as meth.

Lynn smiled and said, "I think torch is going to be pissed."

*

Chapter 29

I was wearing down and we had no idea where Torch was, and no one was talking either. Everyone was frightened of Torch, he really must be a force to reckon with. I found Lynn in the squad room after she had questioned a number of perps with no luck.

"Since this is turning into a bust for finding Torch, I'm going to see what my happy little family is doing and hope there's some food left for me. I'll talk to you tomorrow."

"Thanks, just bale out on us when we are so close," Lynn called after me.

"Only in horseshoes Lynn, only in horseshoes," I said without turning as I walked to the back entrance and out to my van. I sat in the driver's seat gathering my thoughts and then started the van up. I drove home and found my wife and friends in the pool.

"Hey Sweetie, you're home. How was your day?" Penny always made me happy with her greetings. She was so easy going and happy, I just loved the hell out of her.

"Messy, dangerous, and exciting. Shut down some meth labs and brought a drug kingpin to a crashing halt. Unfortunately, we didn't capture the drug kingpin. But there's always tomorrow." I went to the plastic lawn chairs and sat. Willy saw me, climbed up the stairs from the pool and came over shaking water all over my legs. I picked him up and put him on my lap causing a wet stain on my crotch. Oh well, no one would notice.

"If you want some hamburgers, there are some in the fridge from our excellent barbecue earlier. We waited but you had better things to do," she said with a smile.

I sat watching them frolic in the water, Blake having a good time. He reminded me of a teenager just about time for puberty. He had a freshness about him, I probably didn't even corrupt him by having him follow Angelo.

After I went in to nuke a couple burgers in the microwave, everyone came in and Penny said they were going to take Val and Blake back to the MGM. Their wedding was coming soon and they needed to rest up for it.

"Rest? They'll have a whole life to rest. They're in Sin City and they want to rest?" I said.

Penny got close and said, "They aren't really going to rest, they are taking in the strip and the casinos tonight, their last couple nights being single and shameless."

"Oh, I see, well that's different. They don't want to be with us old fogies on their last ditch for freedom."

"That's it Sweetie, now enjoy your food, I'll drive them to the hotel." She went off , Val and Blake said their good-byes and they were gone.

I was alone in the house except for Willy, and it was so quiet. I went into the bedroom, took off my clothes and crawled into the bed. It wasn't that late but it just seemed like a good thing to do. I was passed out before I knew it.

Penny was shaking me to get up; it was morning. I was amazed that I had slept through the night and didn't even have to get up for a middle of the night pee.

Blue Suede Murders

I stumbled to my personal bathroom and forced myself into the shower. About an hour later I was showered, shaved and groomed. I went out to find Penny in the kitchen making oatmeal.

"Isn't Angelo gracing us with breakfast this morning?"

"Nope he had to go to work early, Hollywood types work all hours. So are you going to catch your criminal today?"

"I hope so, just to get this over."

"Why don't you leave it to the police?"

"You know I can't do that, I have to follow it through to the end. That's the way I do things."

"You know you are getting old and may not have many more days ahead, time to take it easy."

"I'll stop when you do." That put an end to the conversation.

Penny was ready to go and said, "I'm picking up Val to go to the studio, it would be nice if you picked up Blake and took him to catch your criminal."

"Tell him to meet me at the valet pickup like before, I'll take him with me, he can keep me company."

Penny kissed me and went off with Willy. I finished my toast and then went to gather my stuff to go out to face the world. I had a decent sleep and was feeling refreshed; hopefully to find Torch today.

I went out to the van and drove to the MGM and picked up Blake. "So how was your rest last night?" I asked when he got in.

"Very nice, we went a little crazy on the strip, won about seven hundred in the O'Sheas' casino. Then we went back to our hotel and celebrated."

"I'm glad you are doing well, Blake. I like you and Val and hope you guys make it. Life's a bitch, just hold on to it."

"Thanks Jim." We were quiet the rest of the way to Metro. We went in to find Lynn and Deacon were not in the office. Warren said that they were in with Weber, I hoped that was good. Blake and I went into Lynn's office and sat.

About ten minutes later, they came back and were surprised to see us. "I thought you probably were taking a pass on the rest of this debacle. We have no more info about Torch than we did yesterday. Any word from your mob friends?"

"Nope and nothing from Earl's contacts either. Maybe Torch packed it in and left town."

"Somehow I don't see that." Lynn's desk phone rang and she answered. She listened and then had a strange look on her face. She said to me, "It's a call for you." She handed me the phone, I held the mouthpiece and told Lynn to put it on speakerphone

221

and then I answered.

"Hello, this is Jim Richards."

"I had a feeling you were behind this, I got the final word from Berlington, just before I set him ablaze. I'm not happy with your intrusion in my affairs. It's bad enough the cops fucked up my business, but I find you stuck your nose in it, well I'll take care of you. Be sure of that," he said and hung up.

I had that same chill again like every time I knew something bad is happening or going to happen. I looked to Lynn, "I guess he knows me. Now what could he do to hurt me?"

My cell phone buzzed and I answered, caller ID said it was Gordy, Penny's producer. I really had that chill now. "Hello, Gordy what is it?" I put my cell on speaker.

"Jim we have a problem. Penny and her friend Val were just grabbed in the studio by four men with guns. The leader had a mask and said that he would kill Penny and her friend if we called the police. He said to call you and tell you to get here now or he was going to shoot Penny one limb at a time before he burnt her to death. I called as soon as they went off to some area in the studio, he said he wanted you here alone in twenty minutes." I said I'd be there and hung up.

Lynn said to follow her; we went to get the Dodge Charger, the fastest car in the motor pool. She waited till we were all in and blasted the sirens and lights. We flew towards the studio and Blake was having fit knowing that Val was taken again.

"Ah don't know if ah can take much more of her being threatened, and she is going to be a wreck."

"Don't worry Blake we'll get her back and Penny, I swear on Torch's head."

Lynn cut the sirens just before we got to the studio; I said I wanted the two of them to hang back. Since they were in civilian clothing, they didn't look like cops but I didn't know if Torch knew what they looked like. We pulled up to the main entrance and blew past the front desk and security; there was no one there.

I found Gordy in the studio where Penny's show was taped. He looked bad.

"They stormed in from the audience entrance and went straight for Penny and Val. They held them and made their demands and went through that door." He pointed to it. "We cleared out everyone from the building to the back lot for now. I know from the two incidences back at the station in Michigan how this goes down."

"Thanks Gordy, now you get out so they can't harm you. We'll take it from here."

I looked to the door where they went, I told to Lynn to wait outside the door until she heard something. She agreed. I chambered a round into my

Glock, Blake pulled his service revolver from his leg holster and put it in his belt behind him and we went in.

I yelled for Torch then I heard a voice calling to me. The door from where the voice came from was marked 'Props'. Boy, this was déjà vu, having chased killers twice looking for Penny in her stations, both in Michigan and now here. I hoped this would come out as well as the last two times.

I went to the door and told Blake to stick close to me. We went in and the room was not well lit. I heard a rather creepy voice saying, "You were told to come alone."

*

Chapter 30

"You've got my wife and his fiancé. I think he deserves to be here. Show yourself asshole." I spoke to the darkness. Blake was too young to look like a cop, and armed.

A light suddenly went on; it was a stage light on a pole that they use to light a stage for cleaning. I saw what I hoped not to see, Penny tied to a chair with duct tape across her mouth. She looked more mad than frightened, that was Penny. I didn't see Val, but there were two men by Penny, one had a mask on and

224

the other had a gun aimed at Penny's head.

"I wouldn't be calling names if I were you. I hold the good cards here." The mask moved as he talked.

"What do you want Torch?" I said.

"Revenge I guess. You really blew my little empire with the raids yesterday, taking down my lab and grabbing the biggest shipment of drugs ever to come into Nevada. Not nice, you cost me every dollar I had. I am real annoyed with you, and I have been since you hounded me back when I worked for Nick North."

That clinched it, he was Wallace!

"Yes Jim, I'm Kris Wallace, we've met before haven't we?" he laughed and moved closer to me but still far enough back to prevent me from strangling the hell out of him. "I'll bet this is a surprise?"

"Not really, I had a feeling it was you, even though I saw you blown up in Nick's Porsche."

"Yes, that was a day wasn't it? I was not believing my good fortunes when I awoke in the desert. You see I was stupid for firing the gun that set off the explosion, but the best I can figure was that the explosion was in front of me and it blew me out the passenger window shooting me out into the desert far enough from all the cops. I landed behind some rocks that covered me. I don't know how long I lay there but the wreck and the cops were gone. I was in tremendous pain from the burns to my upper body and face, luckily my legs were covered by the top half of my body from the explosion so they weren't harmed. My cell phone was still in my pants pocket and it still worked, so I called one of my trusted friends and he came out to get me. I spent six months in a burn unit in California, I told them I was burned in a camp stove explosion, it worked. I had to heal and took the time to arrange for my return to Vegas and make up for your meddling. But you just didn't stop did you?"

"How was it that there was a skeleton in the car, they thought it was you." I asked.

"Jim, don't you remember Nick North's favorite pastime?"

I thought and said, "Pulling practical jokes?"

"Yes, he love scaring people and while the cops and you were chasing me up the highway, I looked back to see a skeleton behind the seats of Nick's car. He had bought it to put in a closet at his house for Halloween. That's what they found, not me."

We heard a good number of gunshots out in the studio, then it was silent.

"Well, that tells me you didn't come alone, my men were watching out in the studio in case you brought the cops with you. Too bad for them. Now you are on your own."

I hoped it was Lynn and Deacon who got the jump on Wallace's men.

"So what now Wallace? You going to burn us all?" I said as I slowly moved away from Blake as he stood next to a table with various tools and equipment used to build and create the flat sets for the shows in the studio. I was taking Wallace's attention from Blake hoping he would take the lead in a few moments by taking out the armed man. Time to grow up Blake, I thought.

"Oh I would really love to see you suffer, like I did out in the desert as I lay there in pain. But if I burn you, you won't suffer long enough, so I'll just burn your dear wife and you can stand and watch her go up in flames." He said as he brought out a strange looking cigarette lighter and opened the top.

I could smell the fuel he must have used on Penny; it was that acetone smell that was used on Petrocelli. It was now or never, I pulled my Glock from my back belt and brought it up and fired at Wallace just as Blake pulled his weapon and shot the armed man taking him out. Unfortunately, Wallace must have seen me move, he quickly backed behind a set flat and my shot missed him. I ran to where he went off and he was gone.

Blake and I went to Penny and I carefully pulled the duct tape from her mouth. "Jim, he has Val in that room over there." She nodded her head towards a door off the side where Wallace must have gone into.

I told Blake to undo Penny and went to the door. The sign said it was a paint room. I entered and carefully looked around the door opening, no sign of Wallace, but the room was filled with flats in various stages of being painted. I entered the room and walked around until I saw Wallace spraying a liquid on Val who was unconscious on the floor.

He had one of those bicycle drinking bottles and squeezing the liquid at her. I yelled and he brought up the lighter and said, "Don't come closer, I'll drop this on her." I moved around bringing his attention away from Val, but he held his hand over her with the lit lighter.

"Wallace, I never thought you were smart, you screwed up the drug deal years ago and you haven't done much better now. You won't get out alive."

"Don't underestimate me Richards, I will still get out," he said as he pulled the mask from his face. It was grotesque, a mass of scarred flesh and missing most of his nose. I had to hold on to my wits seeing it. "See what your meddling did to me! I can't go out in public without this damn mask. It has been my reminder to take care of you. And I will, even if your friend here has to suffer."

If I shot him, he could drop the lighter on Val so held the gun down. He laughed and then we heard something behind him. It was Blake. He was holding a can with paintbrushes sticking out and then flung the can spilling the cleaning solvent from it on Wallace. I watched as the flame from his lighter moved up his arm to his body as he screamed. Quickly his body was ablaze and he flailed around, then he turned and ran blindly into a wall crashing into it and fell to the ground.

Blake went to Val and pulled her away from the flaming body of Wallace. I found a large CO2 extinguisher on the wall and started to hit him with the spray. I heard voices and turned to see Lynn and Deacon come running in followed by Penny.

"Late as always," I said to them. Deacon found another extinguisher and was fanning the flame with it. The fire had been extinguished and Wallace lay dead this time.

Blake was trying to revive Val with Penny's help. Lynn came to me, "You just love getting in trouble don't you, ever think of taking up a new profession?"

"Not on your life, I thrive on this." I went to Penny and Blake who were just bringing Val back to life. I leaned over and said, "You two need a shower." Penny punched me in the gut.

About an hour later, all the employees were back in the studio and Joe Lang was amazed to find out Wallace was still alive, well, really dead now. I explained the skeleton and he laughed.

"You know I never expected it to be a store bought one. The fire must have melted whatever held it together and we found only a few bones left. I'm surprised that it was a real skeleton and not plastic."

"Well Nick never did anything half-assed."

They carted Wallace out in the body bag after he cooled down and Deacon was making the report of the incident with the Captain who came out to see the scene. Blake and Val were sitting on a couple chairs in the main studio and looking happy to be together. Lynn was talking to Penny as I came up.

"So I closed your case for you, I'll send my consultation bill to you."

"Don't be so smug, if it weren't for Blake this may have turned out bad," Lynn said.

I looked to him still fawning over Val, "Yep, send him the fee for the investigation. They'll need it to start their new life."

Later we were all back to our home and I didn't feel like starting the barbecue, I had it with cooked meats for a while. Penny ordered pizza to be delivered as everyone sat in the backyard of our home relaxing. I invited Trapper and Buck with their ladies, Earl and Paula, Lacey and Mac, Lynn, Deacon and I even invited the new girl Tracey.

"Here we are again, after a tough case, all relaxing. I hope we have a few days rest before death strikes again," I said.

Penny smiled and said, "I'm getting used to being kidnapped and tied up. I need some kind of award for it all."

"I'll personally award you later tonight," I said with a smile.

She replied, "I'd rather have it on paper if you don't mind."

Bob Moats

Epilog

Saturday morning came, and we had everyone ready for Val and Blake's wedding. The church was ready to go all decorated by our favorite wedding planner, Shelby Francis and I was happy to give Val away to Blake. Angelo was all ready to be Blake's best man and he looked really good in his tux.

Penny was flitting around checking on last minute arrangements; she should get into the wedding planner business. I peeked out to the chapel and all of our friends and acquaintances were in the pews.

We had Father Tom, who presided over our wedding, preside and he was ready to go. It was a last minute change from the Elvis minister, making Penny happy. He signaled the organist and she stared the march. I took Val up the aisle past everyone and gave her to Blake. I sat next to Lynn and Deacon and watched. Penny was looking so happy standing next to Val, she looked back to me and blew me a quick kiss.

The ceremony went by fast, Val and Blake went out to my mini-limo being driven by Angelo and they went off in a hail of birdseed, at Penny's insistence.

We all went to the MGM Grand where we had a banquet room set up for the wedding reception and had a great time. Later, after all the dancing and celebrating was over and most everyone was leaving, I went to Val and Blake.

"Guys, I hope your life is good and fulfilled." I handed Blake a manila envelope and he opened it. There were two ticket packets for a trip to Greece, where Val told me she was born. There was an itinerary for a travel tour through the countries and ending in England. Val jumped up and thanked Penny and I, and Blake was speechless. I figured he'd be speechless most of his married life but wished him well. I told them their plane left tomorrow in the afternoon, and we would come by to take them.

They finally retired to their room upstairs in the hotel and I took Penny out to the mini-limo. Angelo followed and was going to drive us back to our home. I told Angelo to take a trip up the strip first, he liked the idea.

"I have been so happy being married to you," I said to Penny in the back of the car and she kissed my nose.

"It's been a good couple years for me too," she said with her evil little smile. I pushed the button to put up the privacy shield between Angelo and us.

"Shall we renew our honeymoon night?" I asked.

"You devil you," she said and attacked me.

*

THE END

~~*~~

Enjoy a preview of the next book, Honky Tonk Murders

Chapter 1

"She closed the door, and I just sat there,
Not moving to go and bring her back..
She had enough of my lifestyle, and I can't blame her,
I wouldn't want a man like that."

The country crooner warbled the soulful tune into the mic of the honky tonk bar just off the western edge of Las Vegas. The crowd sat and was mesmerized by his heartfelt words, then the man in the big Stetson hat stopped singing and gave a pained look, then toppled off the stage onto the front tables spilling drinks and food all over the startled customers.

Someone screamed to get a doctor, but it was too late, the country singer was dead.

Two days later on a Friday morning, I was creeping through the dark halls of the Richards Investigations and Security office. It was around five in the morning and I wanted to get in to my office and do a little paperwork. No one else was in at that hour, so I was alone, I liked it that way. I entered my private domain and sat at the new desk that I had delivered last week. It was a nice mahogany and maple carved desk, with big drawers and a couple secret ones that only I knew about. I kept an extra gun in one of them.

I pulled a file and started going over it when my cell phone rang. I looked at the caller ID and saw it was Penny, my main squeeze, wife and Vegas TV talk show host.

"Hey babe what's up, I just left you at the house?" I said into the tiny hole of my cellphone and listened to the slightly bigger hole to hear her reply.

"Jim, I just got a call from my cousin, she's in need of help," Penny said sounding half-asleep.

"Your cousin calls you at five in the morning? What did she want?"

"Her husband died a couple days ago and she thinks he was murdered. She knew I was married to you and living here in Vegas and wanted to know if you could help her?"

"Well, tell her to call me when we open, I'll see what she has and go from there. Now go back to bed and meet me for lunch, just call first."

She said she would and hung up. I sat back wondering why her relative would call so early. I knew this cousin lived in Phoenix, Arizona, she was Penny's only cousin that she ever talked about. The cousin, Jenny Wayne, was married to some rising country singer that had modest record sales on the country charts. I tried to remember the singer's name, but was drawing a blank. The last name wasn't Wayne, that sounded too Yankee, so the singer took on a stage name.

I went back to my paperwork, trying get the cases that had been completed ready for Lacey to file. The last month had been busy for us; we had everything from chasing down missing grooms to foiling industrial espionage for a big pharmaceutical company.

Las Vegas was a good move for Penny and me, I felt. Back in Michigan we had many adventures starting with the infamous classmate murders. I had this strange thing about being followed by murder, and Penny loved to play up that curse. I didn't believe it, but being a private investigator, murder was bound to come up occasionally.

I heard a door open towards the front of the building. I glanced at the digital clock on my desk and it read just before six. Still too early for anyone to show up, I waited as I heard footsteps coming down the hall. I had disabled the building alarm so if it was one of my cohorts, they would know someone was in the building.

Buck suddenly appeared at my door and gave me a big smile.

"Whatcha doing in here so early Jimmy?" the big man asked.

"Paperwork, so we can get paid. What are you doing here so early, as you say?"

"Have to reschedule a few guards at one to the dealerships and call in a few to work. It's been more work than I thought there would be. Back when I was a security guard in Michigan, I used to just sit all night, no cares, now being the boss, just too much work."

"I can understand, how's business?"

"Good, we have over a hundred and sixty guards now, all spread out over Vegas, protecting properties from the bad guys," he said with a smile. "Don't work too hard, I got to make a few calls to get people out of bed to go to work. That's the part I enjoy." He went off to his office, leaving me to go back to my paperwork.

Around seven-thirty, Lacey came bouncing in and said good morning. "You're in early, good, got your end of the month reports ready for me?"

"Yes, boss, I do," I said with a smile and stood to give Lacey the files I had finished. She took them and went back to her desk up front.

I was still standing by my office door when heard her phone ring up front and then heard Lacey's voice over the intercom saying I had a call. I went back to my desk and sat, picking up the desk phone and hit the blinking button.

"Good morning, Jim Richards speaking," I said feeling more awake now.

"Jim, it's Penny's cousin Jenny, did she tell you I called?" came the voice on the phone, sounding like it came from a thirteen-year-old girl.

"Yes, Jenny, she did. You told her that you think your husband was murdered?"

"The police aren't telling me much so far, let me explain. Ricky is my husband, was, and he was in Las Vegas for the big CMA country music awards they have there every year. It's this weekend. He was performing two days ago at some little club in town and they say he just fell over and died. Jim, he was only thirty-one, a person of that age just doesn't just fall over and die. I'm in Phoenix and can't get out there to Vegas, we have a daughter in the hospital with a blood disorder and I have to be here for her. I didn't know what to do, but I remembered that Penny had moved to Vegas and you were a detective. Can you help me find out what is going on?"

"Jenny, let me make a few calls and see what I can find out. You can't come out here at all?"

"No, I'm the only family here and I have to be near my daughter. I really want to be out there but it's impossible."

"Okay, sit tight and I'll be back to you as soon as I can. Now what name did your husband go by?"

"Ricky Lawless, he thought it was a name that would get him some attention, I didn't like it but his agent and the recording company people thought it was a good hook. He was getting popular on the music charts."

"All right, I'll see what I can find out, I'll call you back later today," I said and noted the phone number off the caller ID and she thanked me.

I sat back thinking of how to attack the problem. I could call Lynn Carter and see if she has anything on it, she was homicide and may have something. I reached for my desk phone just as Trapper walked in.

"Hey Jim, what ya working on?" Trapper said then plopped down on my client chair.

"Just come in why don't you."

"Thanks, I'm already in. Got anything exciting?"

"Just finished our monthly reports and I got a call from a cousin of Penny's, seems her country singing husband was in town for the CMA country award show this weekend and he died while performing in some club a couple days ago. She can't come out so she asked me if I could help. I was just going to call Lynn Carter to see if she knows anything about it."

"Lynn is good people. Oh and Earl has flown the coop. He and Paula ran off and went up to the mountains. Seems Paula wanted to get away from all the bright lights and to shake off the big city. The media is still talking about the Elvis murders you know."

"Yeah, it was good that we caught the guy who killed the top Elvis in town and was murdering all the drug dealers. That will make a good book for later. Now do you have anything else to do besides delay me?"

"Nope, just wanted to let you know I was in the area, and will be all day."

"I'll note that in my appointment book, now beat it so I can go to work."

Trapper laughed and stood, "Someday you'll need me." Then he left.

I was laughing as I dialed Lynn Carter. She came on and I told her it was me, asked if she knew about the death of a country singer and gave her the name. She said she did and asked why I needed to know.

"He's a cousin of Penny's, the guy's wife called and wanted to see if I could help. I said I'd see what I could find out. Can you tell me what happened?

"Preliminary report says he died of a coronary attack, which was the ME's initial findings, but Joe Lang isn't so sure, no proof yet, but he's thinking it may have been murder."

*

Continued in the book…

~~*~~

Jim Richards Family of Readers

Thanks to the following people who are now part of the Jim Richards Family of Readers. They have read a book or more and enjoyed them. They all volunteered to be included in the list. If you are a fan of the books, send me your full name and you will be included in future books. Send your name to murdernovels@bobmoats.com to be added here and on the website.

* Achim Feifel * Al Norris * Alex Wheatley * Alexandra Delporte-Wilkinson * Amy Tapia * Andrea Bryan * Anne Shepherd * Arianda Sugar * Arlene Markowski * Ashley Augustus * Audra Hall * Barbara Hughes * Barbara Sammons * Barbara Schuler * Barbara Zirger * Beth Donohue Plenskofski * Betsy Childress * Beth Gibson * Bill Sandy * Bill Tornquist * Billie-jo Collie * Boni J Rychener * Carl Bishopric * Carla Lewis * Carole Henderson * Carolyn Conroy * Carolyn Riddle-Linington * Cassy Bailey * Cathie Turner * Chad Hudson * Charlotte L Duran * Cheryl L. Everett * Cindy Ackley

Blue Suede Murders

Nunn * Cindy Valstad * Connie Bancroft * Corinne Kay O'Daniel * Dana Robbins Chuchran * Dana Wichita * Danielle Monique * Darren Heald * Dave Travers * David Wilkinson * DeAnn Jannereth * Deanna Miller * Deb Breuker Balbo * Debbie Carter * Debbie White * Deborah Fartuch * Deborah Gauze * Deborah Sullivan * Dee King * Denise Freeman * Diana Carver * Dixie Beck * Donna Gould * Donna Thompson * Donny Minter * Doris Kight * Eddie Moore * Eric Walters * Felicia Annette Bradfield * Francine Menor * Gail Chesney * Georgiann Minster * George Conner * Greg Colucci * Hayley Rankin * Harold Garcia * Heidi Arnold * Irma Ranee Coy * Jacqueline Moss * Jan Kimball * Janice Schneider * Janice Spoor * Jennifer Redmond * Jessica Keown-Belous * Jim Beck * Jo Boguslaw * Jo Turner * Joanne Marie Turner * John Peiffer * John Wisbiski * Joseph Wauro * Joyce Stacy * Joyce Trifiletti * Judy Franklin * Judy Travers * Judy Padgett * Julie Heath * Junnahvee Benson * Karen Dahl * Karen Grams * Karen Higham * Karen Kaiser * Karen Meinburg Richwine * Karen Kirkman Parker * Karin Hawkins * Karin Vasvari * Kathleen Donohue Roesing * Kathleen Riddle-Wolfe * Kathy Hinds Moore * Kathy Jones * Kathy Mitchell * Katie Benzler * Kay Burns * Kelly Garcia * Ken Boggs * Keota Rodriguez * Kiera Mccarthy * Kim Estes * Kitty Stolle * Kristie Sciler * Kirsty Stanton * LaLonnie Scallen * Larry Morris * Leann Parr * Lenora Scales * Leslie Marie Jackson * Linda Forester * Linda Ingle Cox * Linda Kennerö * Linda Magill * Lisa Bower * Liz Gibson * Lorraine Wiman * Loretta Alexander * Lynda Bowles * Lynette Lawrance * LuAnn Louttit * Manny Rothman * Marcia Gibson DeWitt * Marie Calder * Marlene Bryan * MaryLouise Kramp * Mary Lynn Gross * Megan Atkins * Meghan Hyden * Melody Cannavan * Michael Carruthers * Michael Dinkens * Michael Vannoy * Michelle Burns-

Mitchell * Michelle Pilcher * Micki Potter * Mike Moats * Mimi Baur * Myrna Hecht * Nadine Sutton * Nancy Ellen Sayre * Natalie Quine * Neena Martin * O'Della Wilson * Pat Pollington * Pat Rohn * Patricia Jarmon * Patricia C Trezza * Patrick Barry * Paul Lawrance * Peggy Davis * Phyllis Bassett * Raylene Matheny * Rebecca Collins Besner * Renee Brumley * Reta Hanna * Reta Moats * Roberta Navarro-Harder * Sally Berneathy * Sally Hubler * Sarah Santos * Satka Nikc * Sharon E. Edwards * Sharon Mangini * Sharon McMillon * Sheena Rawl * Sherry Amstutz * Shirley Alvarez * Shirley Davies * Shirley Williams * Stacie Rowe * Stephanie Conner * Steve Cullen * Susan Haughton * Susan Hesse Adams * Susan Salomon * Suzan K Chase * Taisha Cullum * Tamara Moore * Tammy Castleberry * Tammy Lynn Wood * Ted Murphy * Terri Atkins * Terri Creech * Terry Raab * Tonia Rachael Riggs-Williams * Travis Fleury-Lopez * Twyla Gawlas * Val Brooks * Walt Munsel * Yvonne Isakson *

Thank you to all these wonderful people.

Thank you for purchasing this book. I hope you enjoy it as much as I enjoyed writing it for my faithful readers. Please feel free to email me to tell me what you thought about my stories. I love hearing from the readers. I can be reached at murdernovels@bobmoats.com thanks again!